Cuba's Carnival

Origins of the Biggest Party on Earth

The Companion Book to the Documentary Film *Cuba on Fire*
by
Uwe Blesching

Cuba's Carnival
Origins of the Biggest Party on Earth

ISBN# 978-0-9823570-1-9

Logos Publishing
Berkeley, California. 2010
Copyright © 2010 Uwe Blesching
Unless credits given in picture index, all photos are by author.
Printed in the United States of America

Of Dogs and Stars and Seven Sisters

"...when the powerful force of spring awakens the Dionysian impulses in all of nature the subjective reality disappears into the total forgetfulness of self... and we are truly, if but for a few short moments, one with creation. ...in this Dionysian delight we can catch a glimpse of the incredible, indestructibly, eternal and ancient lust for life at the heart of creation itself."

Friedrich Nietzsche "Die Geburt der Tragödie"

Once upon a time, long, long ago, legend has it that 'Warrior Gods' from the star system Orion, traveling in their 'divine ships' through the vastness of space, had discovered the third planet from the sun. Apparently fascinated with the abundance of life on this watery world they made it a playground for 'scientific' experimentations. They carelessly cloned beasts with that of the primitive humans of that time, just to see what would happen. While the agonizing pains and labored breaths produced by experiments gone terrible wrong echoed up into the endless firmaments, they were neither lost nor left unanswered. Histories recorded the elemental cries of Cyclops, Sphinxes, Centaurs, Medusas, and many other creatures long turned to stone. They are remembered in countless sculptures, in the annals of the world's mythologies and to this day on the magic screens - the movie theatres of 'modern day' man and woman.

Other members of the universe such as those from the blue star systems of the Seven Sister (Pleiades) and the Dog Star (Sirius) noticed these horrible things and would not allow them to go on. They took steps to intervene. Since war and confrontation was not their way they instead engaged in a grand and creative adventure. It started by taking away the source of the energy the 'Warrior Gods' needed to conduct their experiments. Furthermore, it was decided to actively participate in a co-creation that blended their own DNA with that of these earlier humans. The 'Blue Star Adventures' brought love to the table of chaos and creation and engaged the permission and collaboration of the early humans' spirit and soul alike.

As a result of this collaborative spiritual and genetic adventure, humanity rapidly transcended with extraordinary new abilities. Some examples are said to be: the ability to consciously select gene expression; an expansion of the visual spectrum; the awareness of creating one's life experience deliberately; forms of telepathy; the ability to heal oneself or another spontaneously; communication with other realms; extreme longevity; abilities to change ones shape at will; or new and creative means to inspire solutions to all kind of problems.

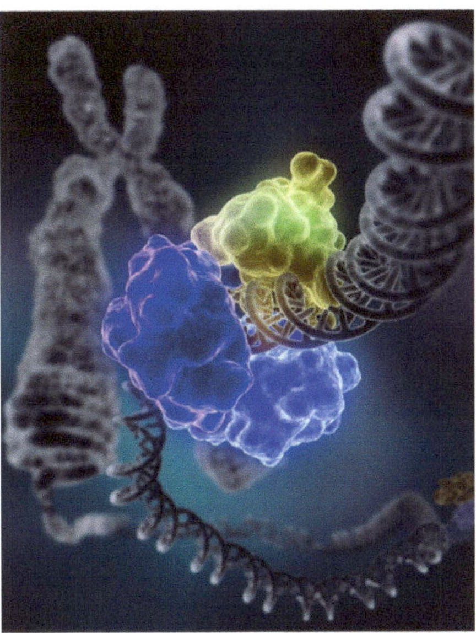

Enzyme based DNA repair

Having been faced with the loss of their energy source and a 'new' humanity with potential abilities similar to that of the 'Gods', the 'Warrior Gods' themselves were effectively robbed of their advantages to continue horrific and loveless activities on Earth. And from their dominator point of view, this co-creative activity between the blue star alliance and humanity was a betrayal of the highest order. The 'snake' had dared to give the 'carnal apple of knowledge' to their 'toy' creatures.

While the 'Warrior Gods' ultimate stranglehold on their 'paradise' may have been lost forever the presence of their methods suggests that this transformation may be an ongoing process in people individually and in humanity at large. History is full with examples of how the forces of careless domination were tempered and ultimately overcome by the powers that creatively produced change without control or hurting anyone. Some say the ancient visitors are still among us exerting influence, some say they are part of who we are genetically and spiritually, and some suggest that both is true.

Truth be as it may, but there is a common pattern emerging from these ancient legends. A pattern imbued with the steps and the qualities of this ancient, collaborative and interstellar adventure.

A pattern that can be found consistently at the heart of a particular celebration that is as old as history herself. Today this festival is known as carnival.

The examination of this pattern common to all the carnivals of he world suggests that the festival may both be a re-enactment of the ancient legends and it may suggests that carnival is also a celebration of the qualities of these ancient 'Blue Star Adventurers.'

These adventurous qualities are demonstrated by the many powerful, sensual and independent female and male creators who remind us that we all have the power to cre-

ate the life we want to live without control or domination. In Carnival everybody is free to be who they want to be, free to dream and to re-invent themselves with new and expanded abilities; as fools and flowers, kings and queens, spirits, animals, fabled creatures, martyrs, warriors, magicians and adventurers; dancers, virgins, lovers or happy hookers. You decide and you make it so.

To examine the pattern we begin in distant history. Six thousand years ago the 'black headed people', or Sumerians, celebrated a festival called Akitu (A.KI.TU. = 'on Earth create life') that echoes the earlier legends. Akitu commenced at the spring equinox and was celebrated for eleven to twelve days in the month of Nisannu, corresponding to the Northern hemispheric spring months of March and April.

Located between the rivers Euphrates and the Tigris, these Sumerians celebrated in an organized chaos, singing and dancing, climbing on board ships to embark on a journey along the river through the city of Babylon in specifically prescribed and meaningful steps. And what was the meaning for the paradoxical procession of order and chaos?

Sumerian records indicate, that the ancient festival was a celebration and enactment of a group of Annuna or Annunaki - the fifty

great Gods of Sumerian mythology - leaving their planet in a 'divine ship' on their journey to Earth. Their consequent efforts focused on creating new humans to take as workers and mates, and on the many offspring, trials and tribulations, rebellions, wars, and the desire for self-determination that such endeavors do tend to entail.

These myths suggest that some of the Annuna 'Gods' sided with the humans while others did not. Perhaps this is why so many nations go to war in the name of their God. Be that as it may, the festival was said to be a celebration of the creation of a new reality, a new beginning and by the same token the passing of another, just like winter must die to give birth to spring. This transition was also marked by the paradoxical themes of orgiastic chaos, death, birth and intense and often unpredictable changes.

During Akitu, many ships mirroring the travels of the 'divine ship' embarked on a symbolic journey along the Euphrates. Some were eventually pulled up from the riverbanks, loaded onto chariots, and dragged through the streets while the celebrations intensified. One possible origin for the word Carnival may be found in the Latin, 'Carrus navalis,' or ship wagons.

Innana, Babylonian Goddess of the Night

Songs containing tender and frivolous lyrics alike were dedicated to a Goddess, the Lady of the Night, the moon, love and sensuality, battles, and of health and healing. Her name was Innana, later Ishtar. Her powers were connected to felines, and she was described as the epitome of beauty with a strong and independent sexual appetite and a disapproval of monogamy. The sexual celebration of life was one of her means of transcendence:

> *She is clothed in pleasure and love.*
> *She is laden with vitality,*
> *charm, and voluptuousness.*
> *Ishtar is clothed in*
> *pleasure and love.*
> *She is laden with vitality,*
> *charm, and voluptuousness.*
>
> *In lips she is sweet;*
> *life is in her mouth.*
> *At her appearance rejoicing*
> *becomes full.*
> *She is glorious; veils are thrown*
> *over her head.*
> *Her figure is beautiful;*
> *her eyes are brilliant.*
>
> *She dwells in, she pays heed to*
> *compassion and friendliness.*
> *Besides, agreeableness*
> *she truly possesses.*
> *Be it slave, unattached girl,*
> *or mother, she preserves (her).*
> *One calls on her; among women*
> *one names her name.*

Ishtar's priestesses would later in 'herstory' engage in sexual union with 'suitable' males as a means to commune with her and to share the grace of the goddess. Often this included those who could afford it, which might explain why much later the Bible calls her "The Mother of Harlots."

Ancient temple priestesses dedicated to Ishtar enjoyed a high social status, were educated, well versed in the healing arts, sexually independent and powerful in their own right and might have even become queens. These sacred 'harlot' myths are found in almost every culture, and certainly in any Carnival. With the rise of 'warrior gods' patriarchies and the destruction of Goddess-based values, the sacred became the prostitute, and all things sexual became the opposite of being 'spiritual.'

Yellamma, a Hindu 'death and resurrection Goddess,' to this day has devadasis, women dedicated to the Goddess who also in times more ancient were highly respected, educated, artisans and dancers, serving the Goddess in many ways. One practical expression of how the Goddess took care of her devotees was through the sexual union of the temple priestess with those men who could afford this service. An excerpt from a collection of 500-year-old South Indian poems discovered in the famous Tirupati Temple called "When God is a Customer" states:

Again, like with so many other civilizations before the devadasis, came the rise of patriarchal values and the sacred all but disappeared from temples services of old. Survival-motivated prostitution with all its horrors filled the void. Some Hindus today want to see a return to the dedicated daughters of Yellamma of old where a devotional service takes the center stage in the life of a devadasi.

Predated perhaps only by the legend of Tiamat and Abzu (Enuma Elish), Innana and her counterpart Dumuzi (Tammuz) were one of the earliest versions of this passionate dance of life, death and resurrection myths. These 'original' mythologies were later re-created by those of Osiris and Isis, Kali and Shiva, Dionysus and Semele, Attis and Cybele, Adonis and Aphrodite and that of Jesus and Mary (Magdalene). Myths of mothers and sons, myths of male and female lovers tenderly entwined in the eternal and chaotic passions in the heart of creation itself all seem to be a part and parcel of much of our shared humanity.

On the fifth day of Akitu, the King received a slap in the face, was stripped of his authority for the day, and entered a reversed confession in which he must assure that he neither violated what was considered holy, nor the privileges of the citizens of the Sumerian Nation.

> *"To hug me tight,*
> *to touch my place of love,*
> *and get to total union,*
> *listen well,*
> *you must bathe me*
> *in a shower of gold."*

These three themes are customs found in carnivals throughout history and today: orgiastic celebration of the cycles of change, divine ships on land, and reversing the powers that be, if but for a day. Another potential origin of the word Carnival is related to the

Latin, 'Carne vale' - farewell flesh, letting go of the old self and being reborn to a self more akin to what most humans would likely dream themselves to be. This reflects in Carnival as more carefree, more creative, successful, uninhibited, fun-filled and joyful.

Two thousand years after the first record of Akitu, the Father of History, Herodotus, describes a similar ancient celebration; only this time in Egypt. His eye-witness report of the largest of the processions known in Khemet (Egypt) at that time was held along the Nile and at the city of 'Bubastis', located near modern day Zagazig in the Eastern part of the Nile Delta.

Hundreds of thousands of people gathered in honor of a Goddess whose name 'Buto' is contested by historians. Herodotus assumed it to be a daughter of Osiris and Isis. However, historians have no record of a daughter between these Gods. The name Buto is Greek for the Egyptian spiral shaped serpent goddess Per-Uatchet or Wadjet who is often depicted with a woman's head and wings. Considered to be 'protector and mistress' to the gods, she is associated with the source of creation and health and healing. To this day, Caduceus serves as the symbol for the 'modern allopathic' healing arts.

Herodotus writes his eye-witness report from the Nile delta 2,500 years ago: *"Men and women come sailing all together, vast numbers in each boat, many of the women with castanets, which they strike, while some of the men pipe during the whole time of the voyage; the remainder of the voyagers, male and female, sing the while, and make a clapping with their hands. When they arrive opposite any of the towns upon the bank of the stream, they approach the shore, and, while some of the women continue to play and sing, others call out loud to the females of the place and load them with abuse, while a certain number dance, and some standing up and uncover themselves. After proceeding this way all along the river course, they reach Bubastis, where they celebrate the feast with abundant sacrifices. More Barley wine (most likely beer) is consumed at this festival than in all the rest of the year besides. The number of those who attend, counting only the men and women and omitting the children, amounts, according to the native reports, to seven hundred thousand."*

Ancient Egyptians marked the beginning of their year by the rising of the Nile waters. The annual floods brought the time of destruction as well as the rich soil and silt washed by torrential rains from the Ethiopian mountains and Sudanese highlands. This annual flood was the reason for the ever-fertile grounds of the Nile Valley civilizations. In those days long gone it was announced by the new year's first rising star just before dawn. This corresponds to today's July 23, Sirius rising.

The year and life itself renewed; a time for new beginnings. 'Star light, star bright, first star I see tonight, I wish I may, I wish I might have the wish I wish tonight…' Sirius, the brightest and most blue of all the stars in the night. 'Out of the blue,' out of a wish, born of one's desire, as if by magic.

The 'blue' star system Sirius is also referred to as Canis Majoris, or the 'Dog Star', which is referenced in numerous legends and myths from virtually all parts of the world where it is often considered the source of all life. Twin suns (stars) Sirius A and Sirius B comprise the Sirian system. One circles around the other, which is why it seems to twinkle. It plays a prominent role in many of the ancient civilizations such as Sumer and Egypt. Anu was the name of the Sumerian God of heaven, which corresponds to the later Egyptian Anubis depicted as a human body and with the head of a dog or jackal. While Isis, the goddess of fertility, magic and life is rep-resented by the bright Sirius A, the darker and smaller Sirius B might be associated with Anubis, the God taking care of the dead reflecting the ancient interplay of constant growth, becoming, constant change, the death of the old, and the birth of the new.

Sirius is also at the center of the spiritual traditions of the Dogon tribe of Mali who hold that the 'Nommo,' 'merman and merwomen' from Sirius, visited them long ago for reasons they have kept secret from outsiders for thousands of years. The Dogon hold the belief that it is actually a triple star system, perhaps to be discovered again in the future by modern astronomers. Every culture, but especially sea faring ones, has given Sirius a special place in its mythology because it is the star that helps in navigating towards 'home.'

Other world legends similarly describe Sirius as the gateway 'home' in the ultimate adventure to consciously reunite with the source of all life. An Ethiopian belief holds that when all the dogs in the neighborhood howl, some-one died, and a soul is 'returning home.' Indeed, fire trucks, police cars and ambulances driving with sirens howling to an emergency, set off neighborhood dogs, perhaps sensing that someone is about to begin that ultimate adventure echoing the old Ethiopian belief.

Many African tribes, such as the Dogon, trace their origin to that of ancient Egypt and its rich, mysterious heritage. It is perhaps no wonder that today's Carnivals echo themes not just from six thousand years ago, but also with

legends recounting times even more ancient.

Perhaps these customs traveled with the many slaves that were forced to migrate to the Caribbean and the Americas. Yet, maybe it recalls an earlier deposition of these traditions with the migration of the Olmec, the mysterious, partly black featured immigrants to central Mexico around 1500 B.C. Perhaps this tradition reflects part of our genetic, cellular and unconscious memories of timeless experiences uninterrupted.

Not that long ago, people and entire civilizations made sense of the world through nature. Many people today may not realize it or take it for granted because it is so 'natural' and omnipresent. The sun gives the light by day. The moon gives light by night. Both contribute to create a sense of time with all its repeating cycles of creation from seed, growth, flower, harvest and death.

In one of the many historically recorded and still operating calendars, the 'Old English lunar calendar,' spring, summer, autumn and winter fell within the 13 months of the lunar cycle and comprised 28 days each. This Calendar was called 'a year and a day,' because $13 \times 28 = 364$ plus one day $= 365$. People following the lunar calendars saw the moon pulling on the water of the seven seas thus creating an ebb and a flow. They knew the moon was one with the tides of fertile women who felt connected to the power of creation and the stellar bodies. The moon was the triple goddess: the maiden, the mother, and the crone; the new moon, the full moon, and the disappearing moon, respectively.

June 20-21
Summer solstice
Midsummer
St. John's Eve
Litha

August 1
Lughnasadh
Lammas
Procession of the cross

May 1
Walpurgis Night
Beltane
Bona Dea

September 22-23
Fall Equinox
Shūbun no hi
St. Mathew Feast Day

March 20-21
Spring equinox
Nowruz
Sham El Nessim
Shunbun no hi

November 1
Day of the Dead
All Saints Day
Samhain
Halloween

February 2
Imbolc
Groundhog Day
Yemanjá
Candlemas

December 21-22
Winter solstice
Midwinter
Yule
Christmas

Divide the year of the sun into four parts, equal to each other, forming a cross and the divisions of winter, spring, summer and fall. The four parts are specifically marked by the equinoxes and solstices of which the two most celebrated today are Christmas (winter solstice = beginning the re-birth of the sun) and Easter (spring equinox = birth of spring). The tradition of Easter is a continuation of the 'Pagan' nature celebrations for the voluptuous Teutonic goddess Eostre, usually depicted as surrounded by symbols of birth, spring, fertility, and new life. She is the governess of time and change, also translated as death and destruction, depending on one's point of view. Eostra is an equivalent to the Indian Hindu Goddess Kali. An interesting element includes the religious festivals of Easter and the Indian Holi, always beginning on the first Sunday after the first full moon following the spring equinox.

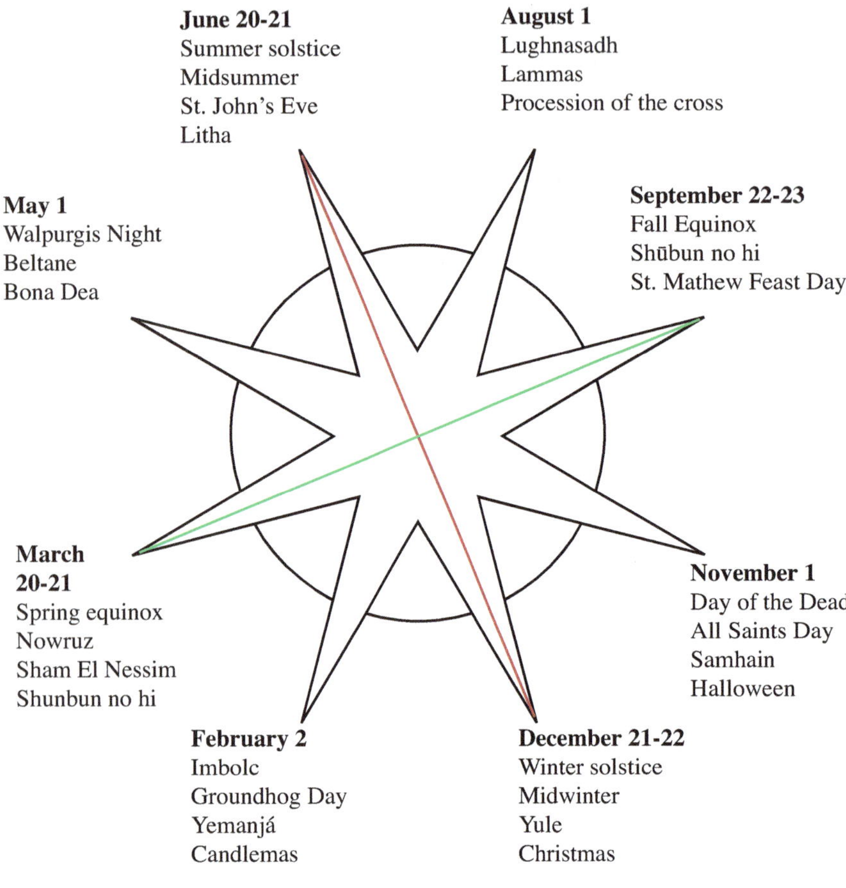

The Holi festival is a virile celebration of the death of winter and emergence of spring and begins with the symbolic burning of the 'demoness Holika.' A special drink is prepared, which sometimes contains bhang (marijuana). Holi has been celebrated for more than 4 millennia. Today, as ages ago, it is a festival of trickery where people throw colored water or dye on each other, so that by the end of the day everybody is covered in "the color of new life." In days not too long ago, the colors were derived from flowers and trees that had cosmetic and medicinal values derived from the neem

tree, and other medicinal plants. The properties of the plants were known to protect the skin. They also contained antimicrobial agents, which may have contributed to a reduction in vector borne illnesses common during this time of the year. However, with the decimation of much of the local flora, the natural dyes have been replaced by chemical versions now discovered toxic for people and the environment alike.

The ancient Greeks celebrated Carnival through their mythologies of Dionysus and Semele. The Romans celebrated Carnival based on their version of the orgiastic cult of Attis and Cybele.

Romans called this day the 'Day of Joy;' it was the day of Carnival, the day of Hilaria, a word still living in today's 'hilarious.' Romans danced and frolicked in the streets wearing masks and engaged in sex, and other things creative and pleasurable without any fear of reprisal. Of course today's Greeks and Romans know how to evoke the resurrected spirit of creation and celebrate Hilaria, or Apokria in Greece, where especially the carnivals in Venice and Patras have become living time machines.

Multiply the four quarters or seasons of the year by two and you will create eight equal parts. These eight points in all are all exactly based on the movement of the sun as he completes his annual journey. These eight points in time are the basic foundation for most non-political holidays that are and have been celebrated by many names throughout most cultures and all of history. Some of those most commonly celebrated are Candlemas (Groundhog Day, the Irish Imbolc festival, Feast of the Purification of the Virgin, Meeting of the Lord) and the Day of the Dead (All Saint's Day, All Souls Day, Day of the Skulls, Halloween).

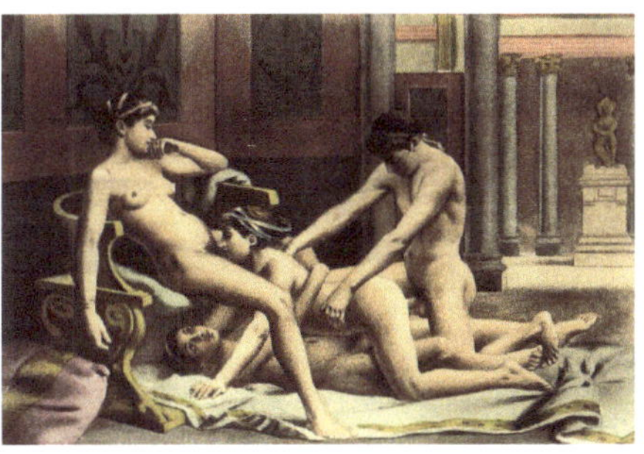

Multiply the four parts or seasons by three and the result will show the sun's 'twelve companions' with which he traverses the sky.

They are also known as the twelve constellations of the Zodiac or the twelve months of the year, the twelve Olympians and so fourth. These mathematical and celestial divisions are but a few examples of how ancient and modern people alike used the movements of the stars as meaningful, complex, and practical means toward a better understanding of time, change, nature and all things considerd to be spiritual. Almost any carnival from any country around the world, from any culture, and almost from any time in history hold similar themes and connections.

Santiago de Cuba

As a litmus test, let's look at one of the more rare and unique expressions of a Carnival, which few outside of the island nation of Cuba have ever been able to experience - the blending colors and ancient themes of the Carnival in the city of Santiago de Cuba. Santiago de Cuba, located in the southeastern part of Cuba, is the island's second largest city. Upon its founding in 1514, Diego Velasquez named it after the Spanish Saint and military Patron, St. Jago, or Santiago (St. James). She is secretly referred to as Cuba's real capital because she was the capital from 1524 to 1549 and is without a doubt, the capital of rebellion and music. Over a half million African slaves arrived in Cuba - most of them in Santiago de Cuba - with their rich and varied internal worlds. Today, this city, like Sumeria of old, continues to reveal 'herstory' in the ebony faces of her people.

(Written in 2010)

If Legend is True, then Carnival is...

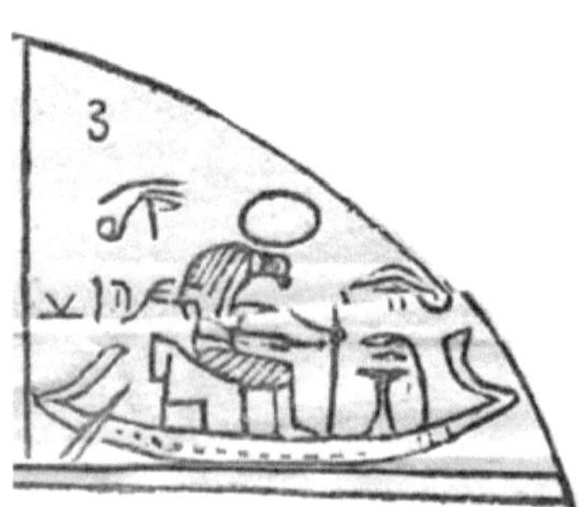

THE MARDI GRAS—NEW ORLEANS.

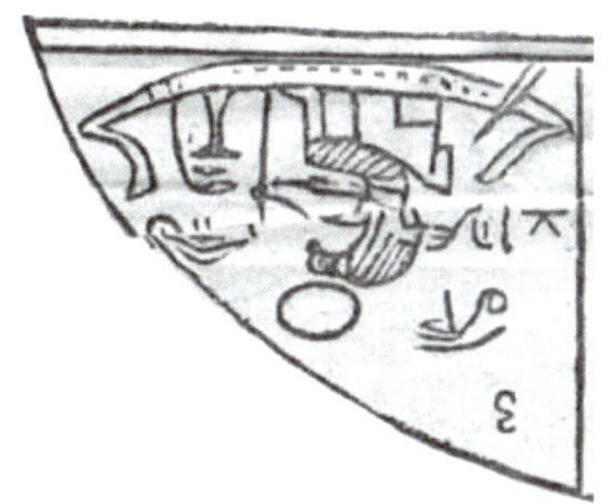

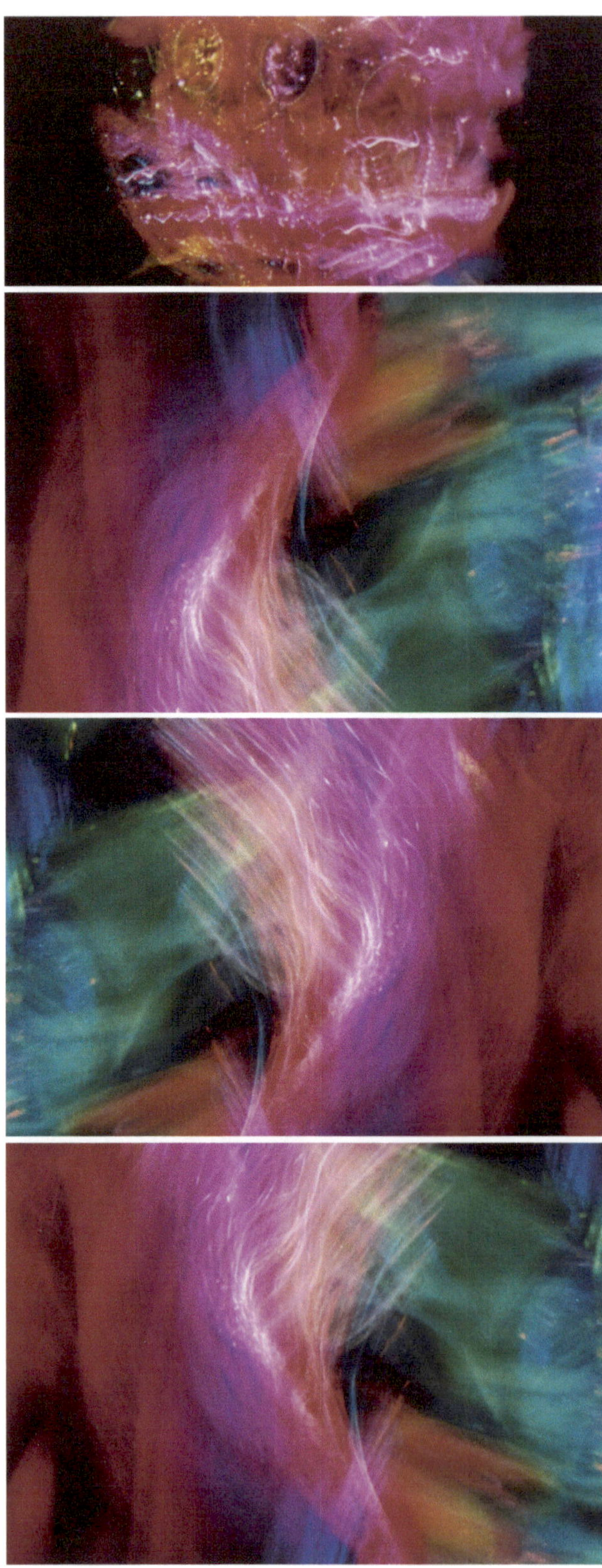

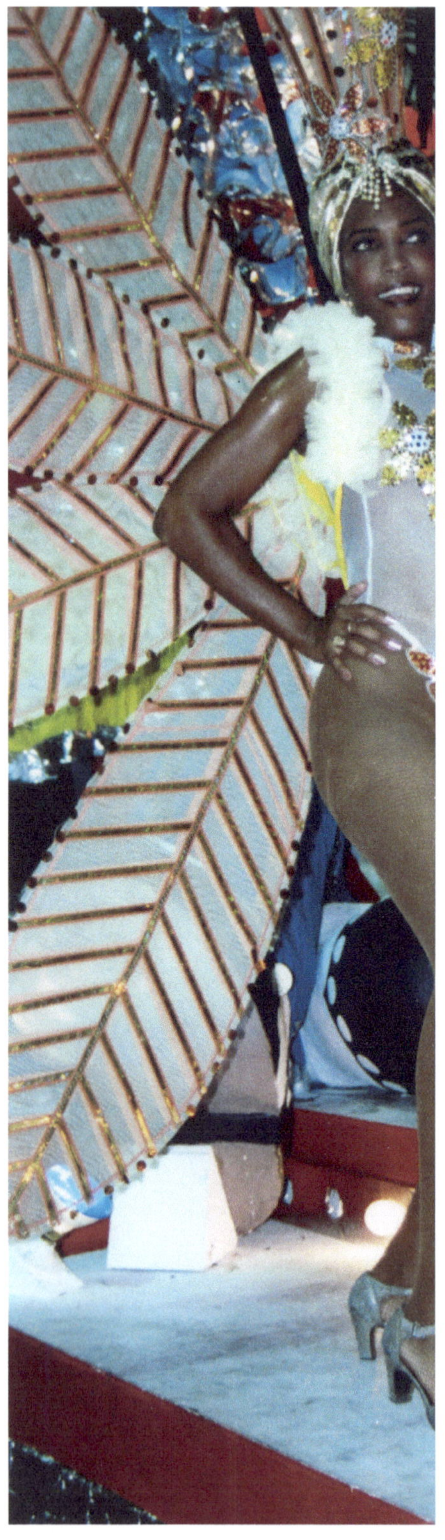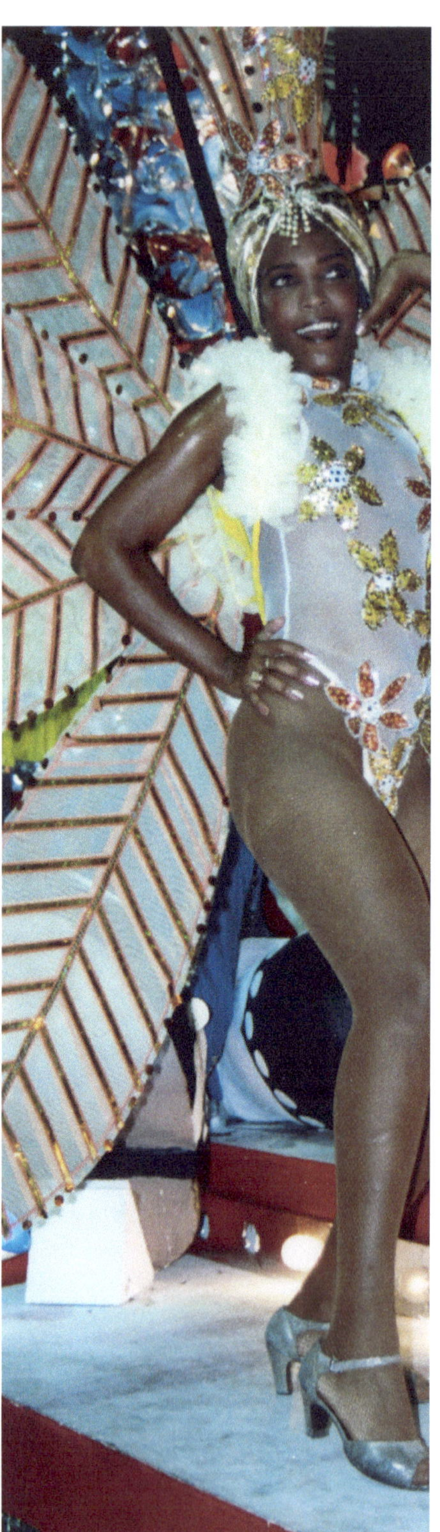

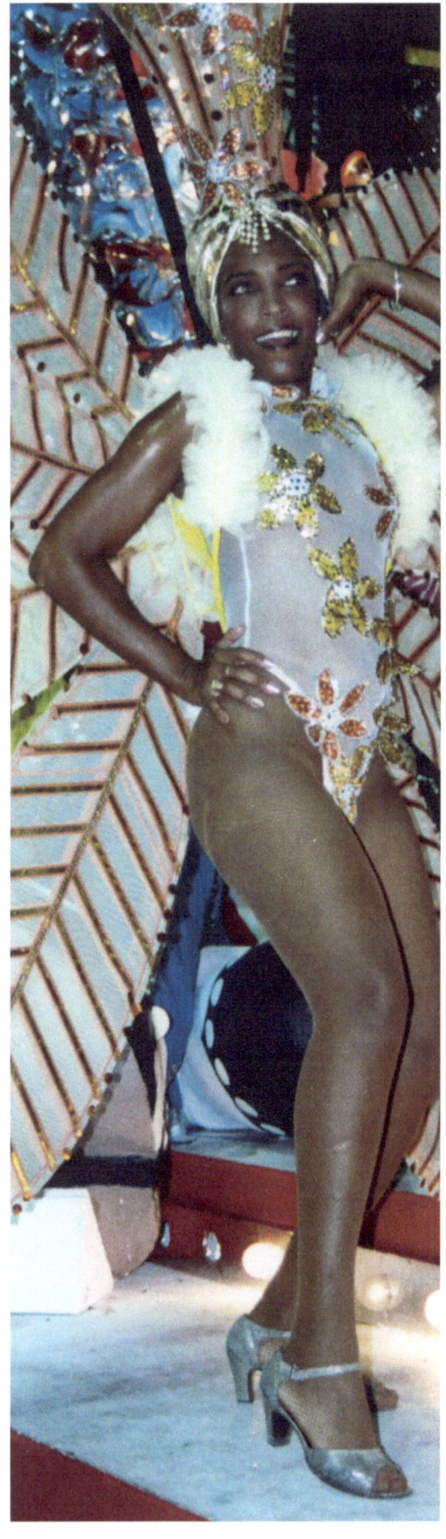
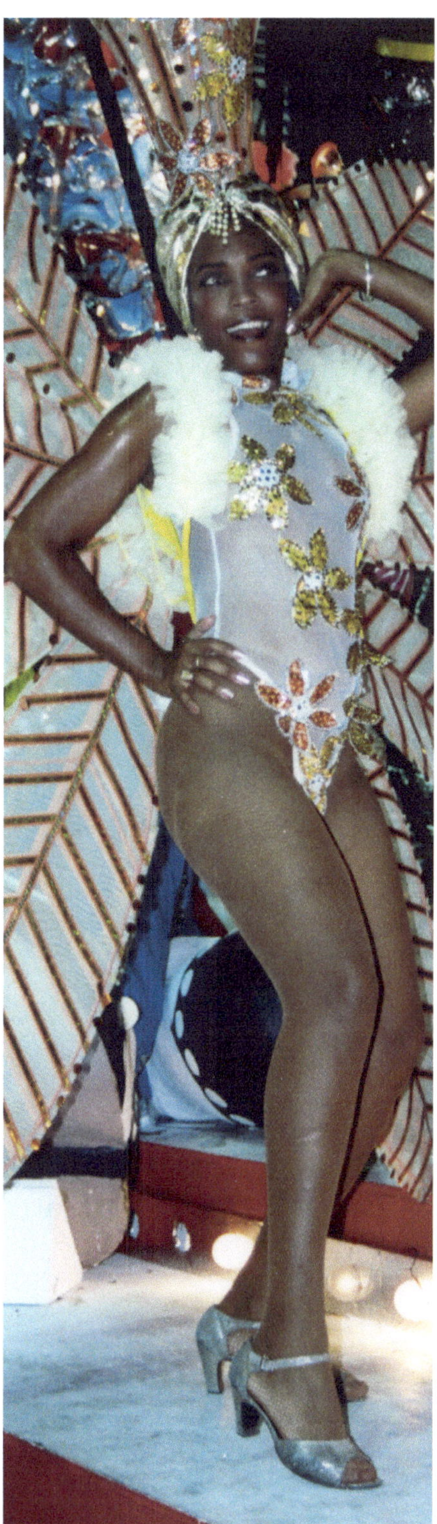

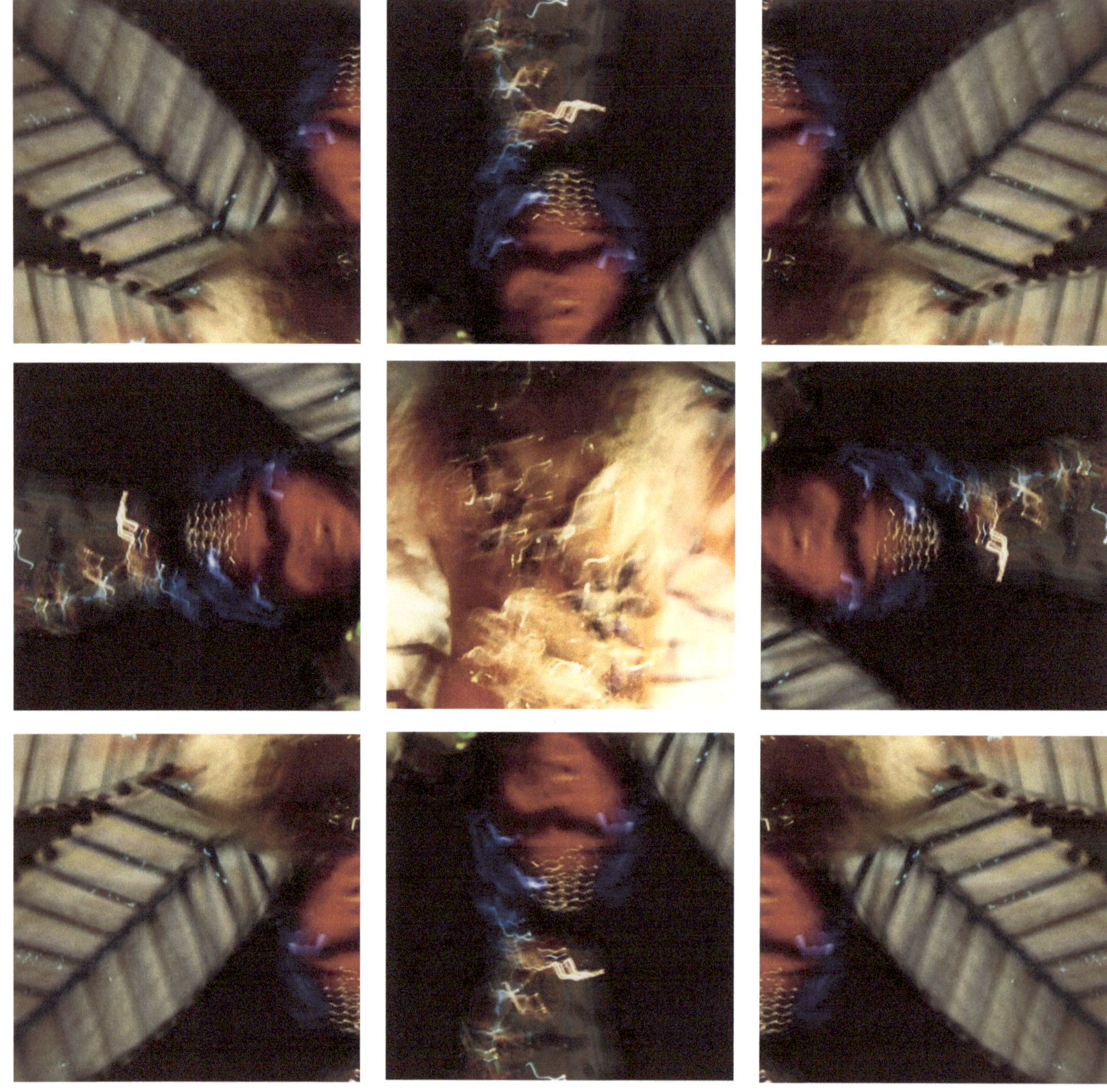

...a challenge to and a shift in the powers that be...

...the arrival of the seven sisters navigating the divine ships through chaos and creation...

If Legend is True, then Carnival is...

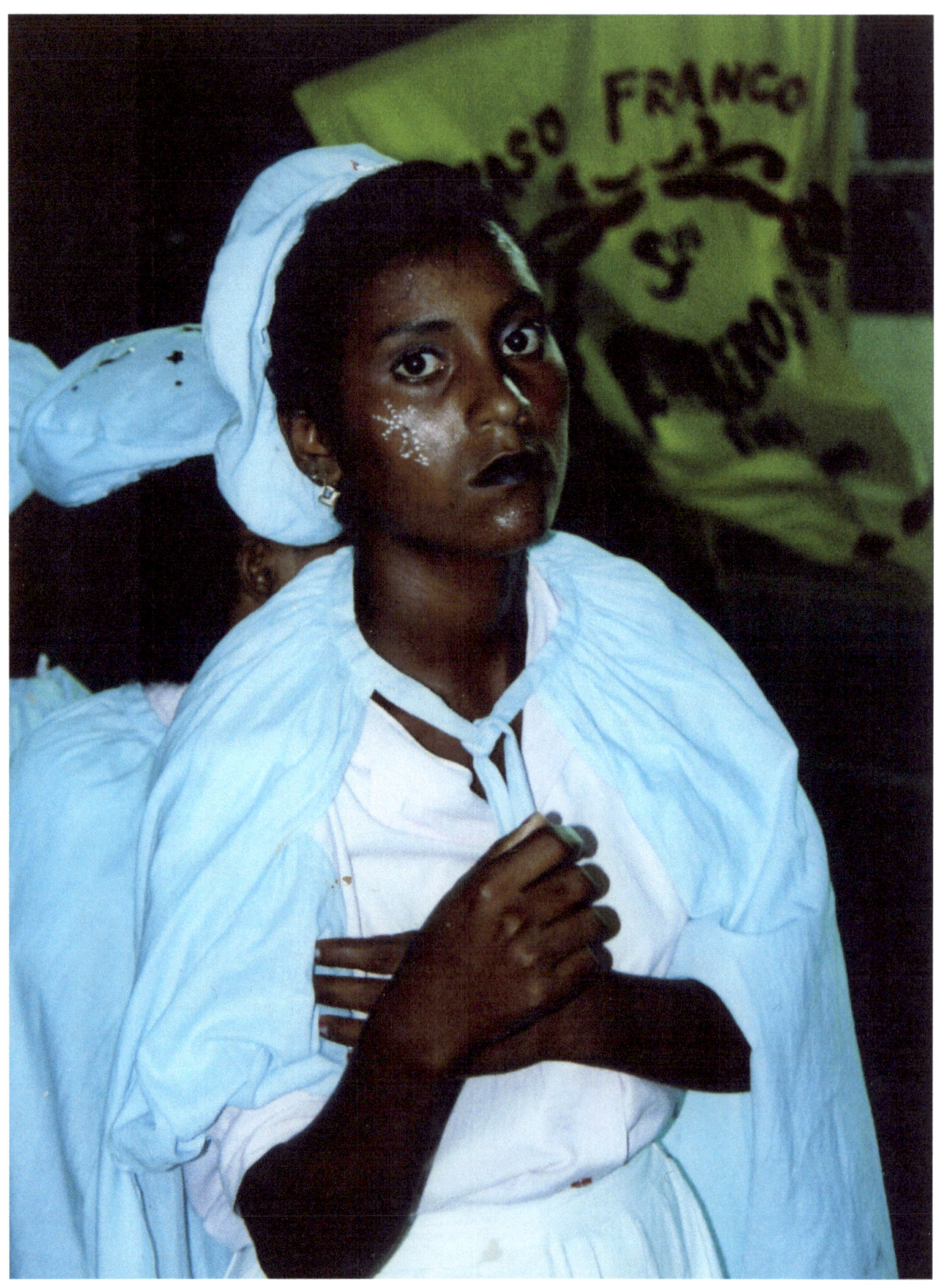
PASO FRANCO
y

† 🪓

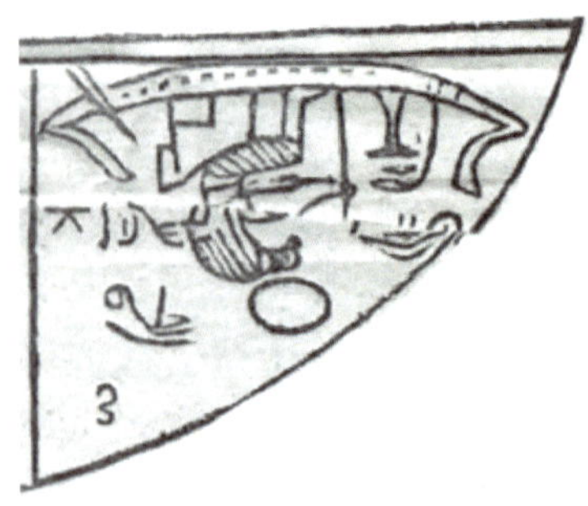

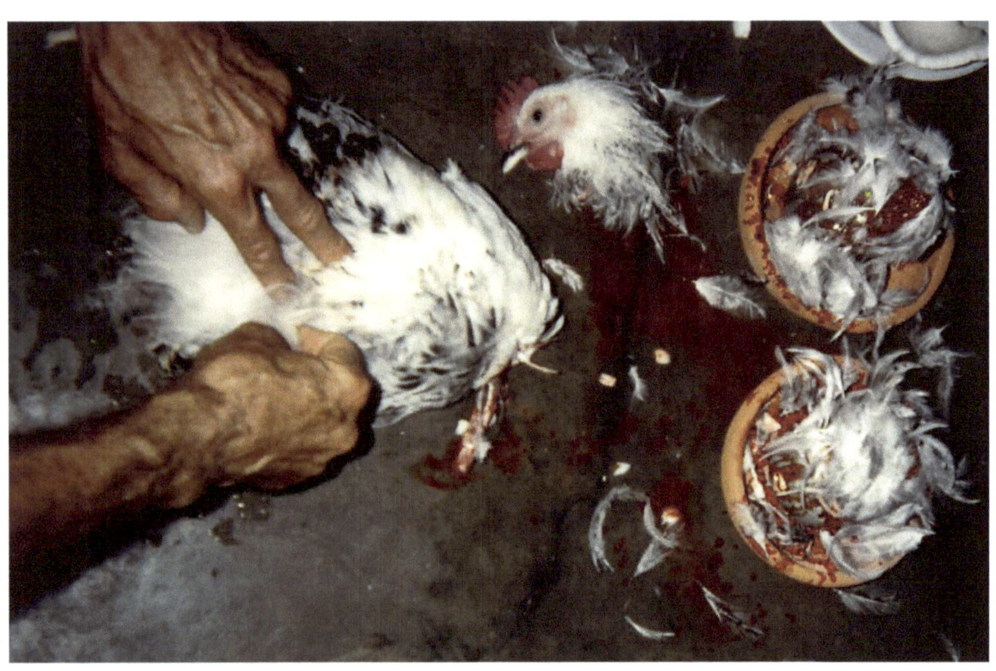

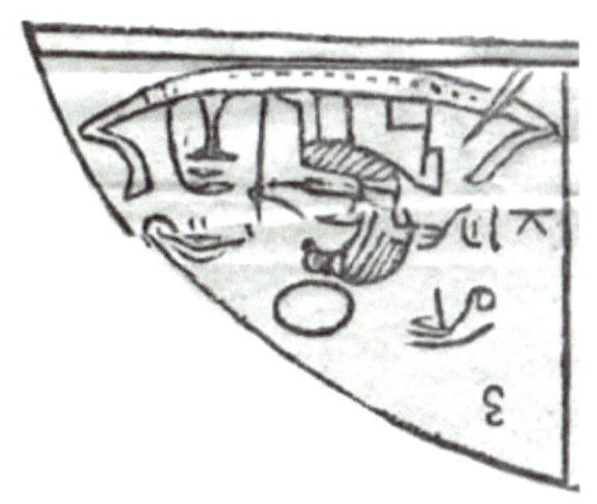

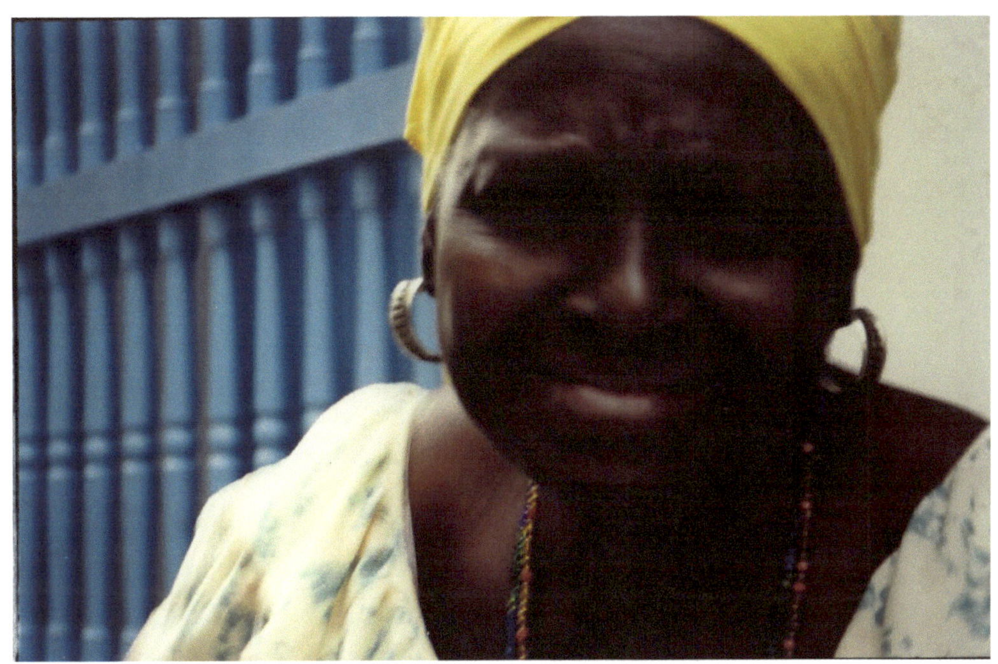

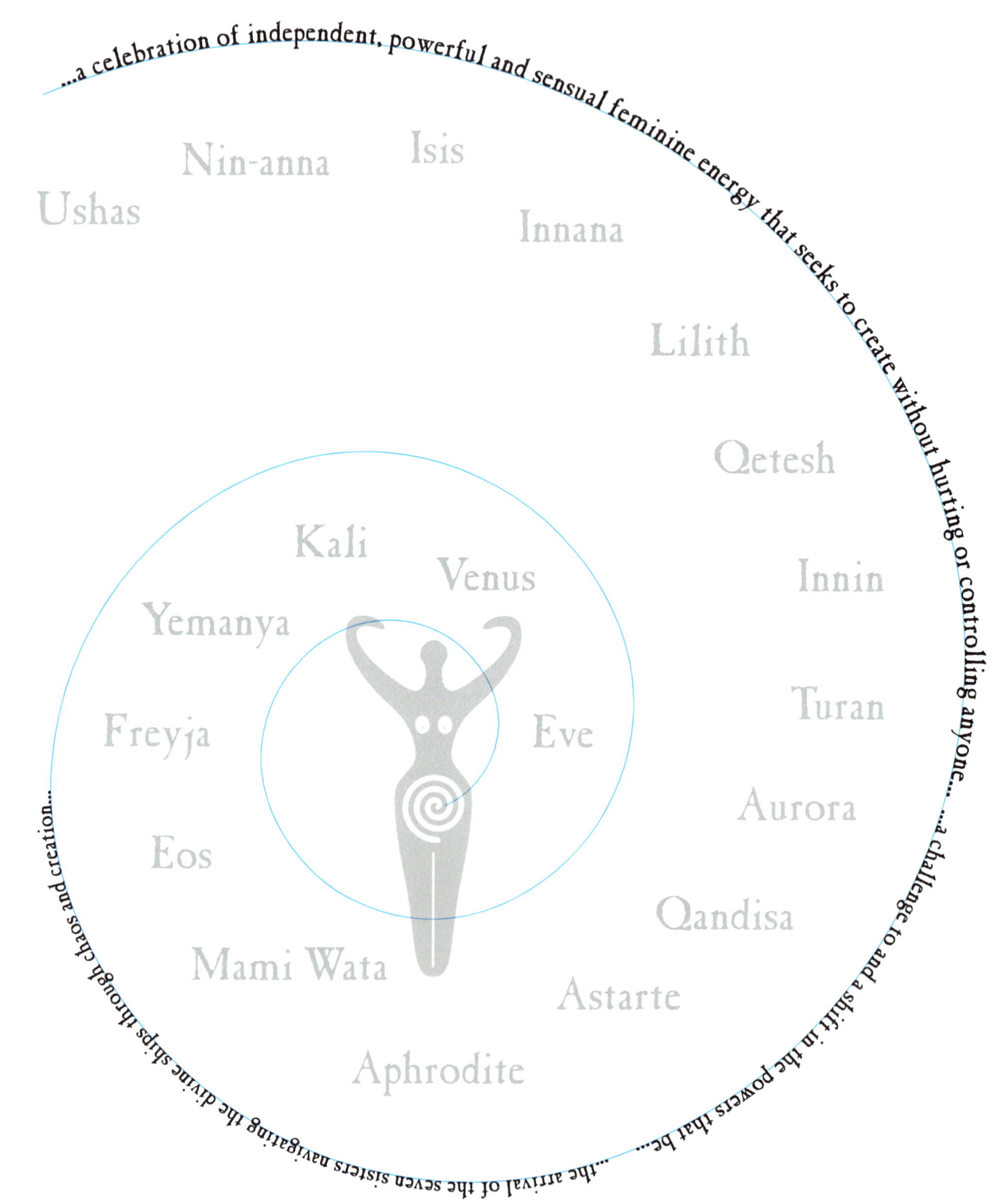

...a celebration of independent, powerful and sensual feminine energy that seeks to create without hurting or controlling anyone... ...a challenge to and a shift in the powers that be... ...the arrival of the seven sisters navigating the divine ships through chaos and creation...
Nin-anna
Isis
Ushas
Innana
Lilith
Qetesh
Kali
Venus
Yemanya
Innin
Eve
Freyja
Turan
Eos
Aurora
Qandisa
Mami Wata
Astarte
Aphrodite

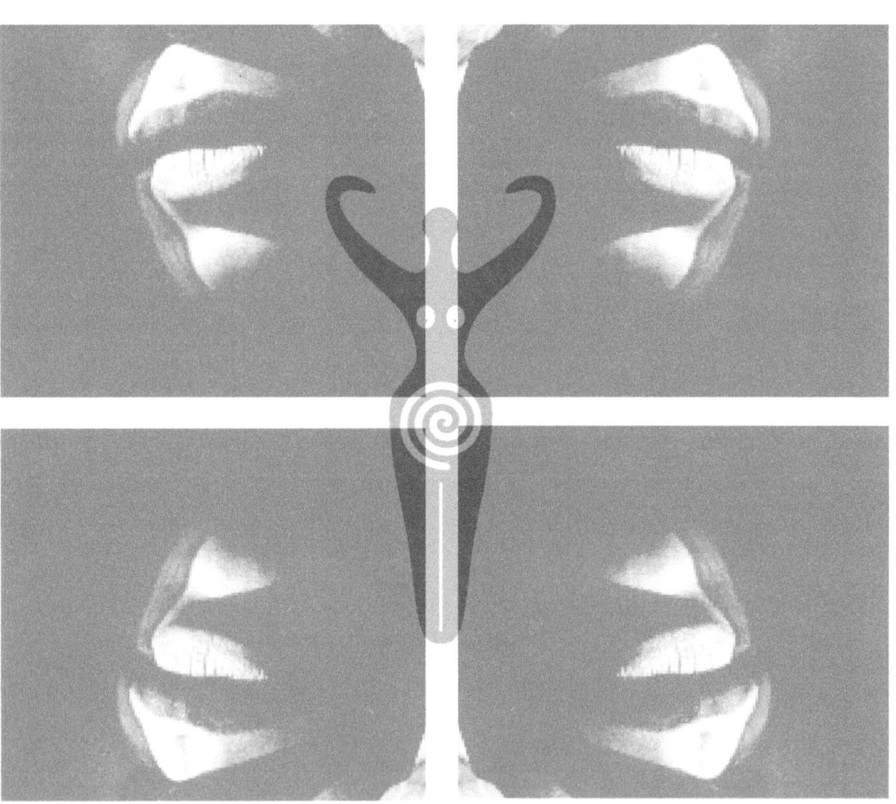

If Legend is True, then Carnival is...

...a reminder that the source of creation resides within... ...a celebration of independent, powerful and sensual feminine energy that seeks to create without hurting or controlling anyone... ...a challenge to and a shift in the powers that be... ...the arrival of the seven sisters navigating the divine ships through chaos and creation...

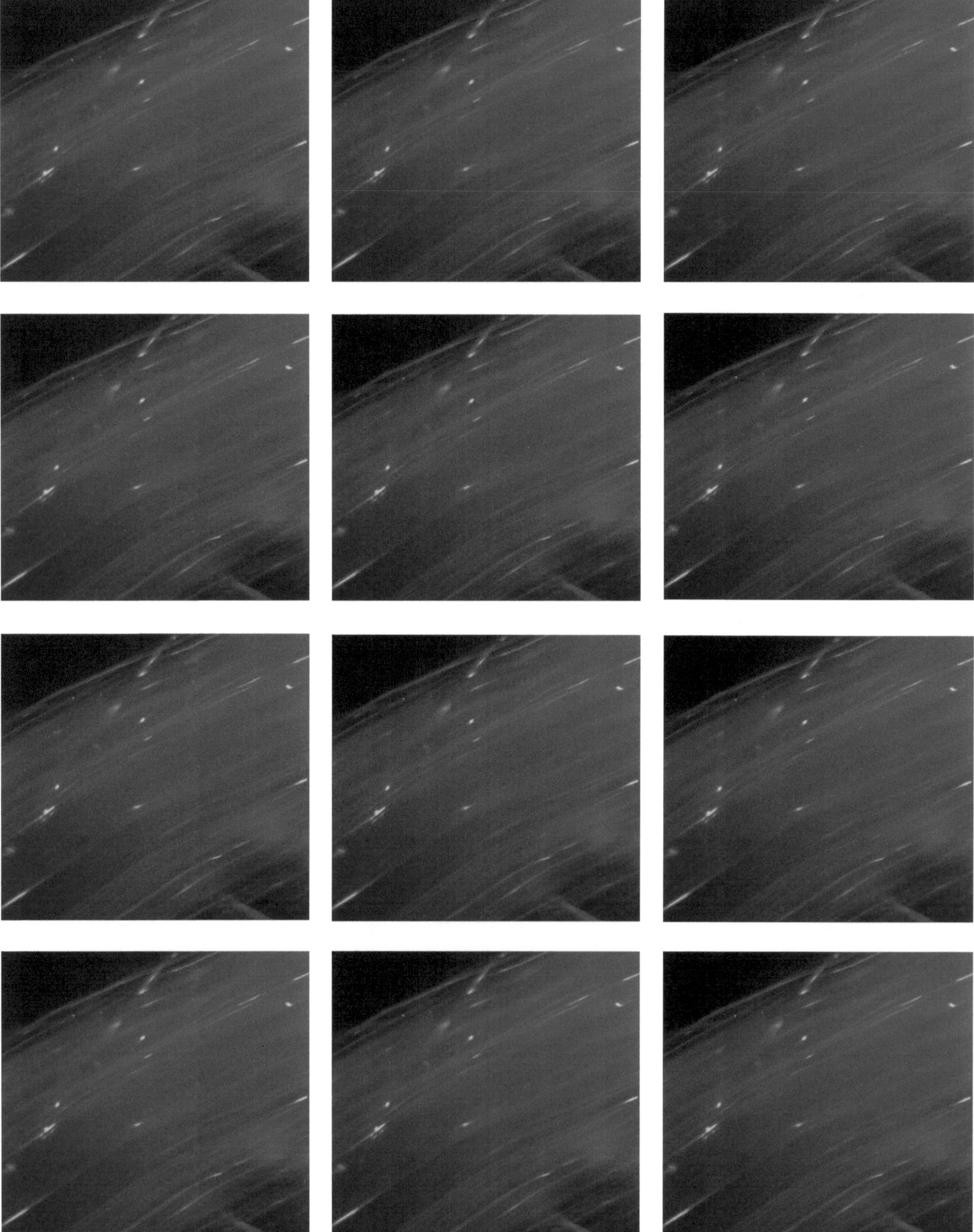

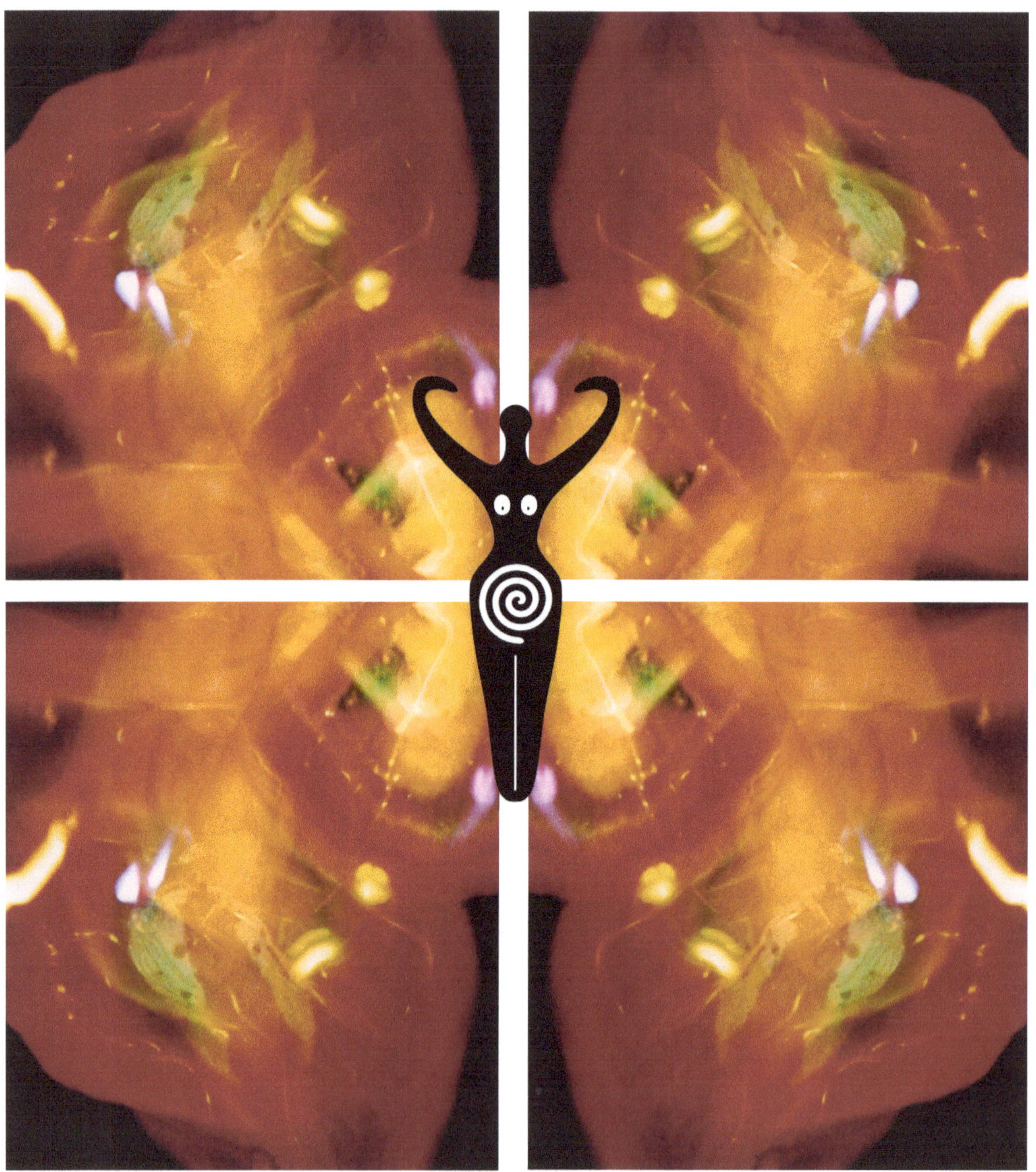

...orgiastic chaos and creation that will not be contained but can be directed......a reminder that the source of creation resides within......a celebration of independent, powerful and sensual feminine energy that seeks to create without hurting or controlling anyone......a challenge to and a shift in the powers that be......the arrival of the seven sisters navigating the divine ships through chaos and creation...

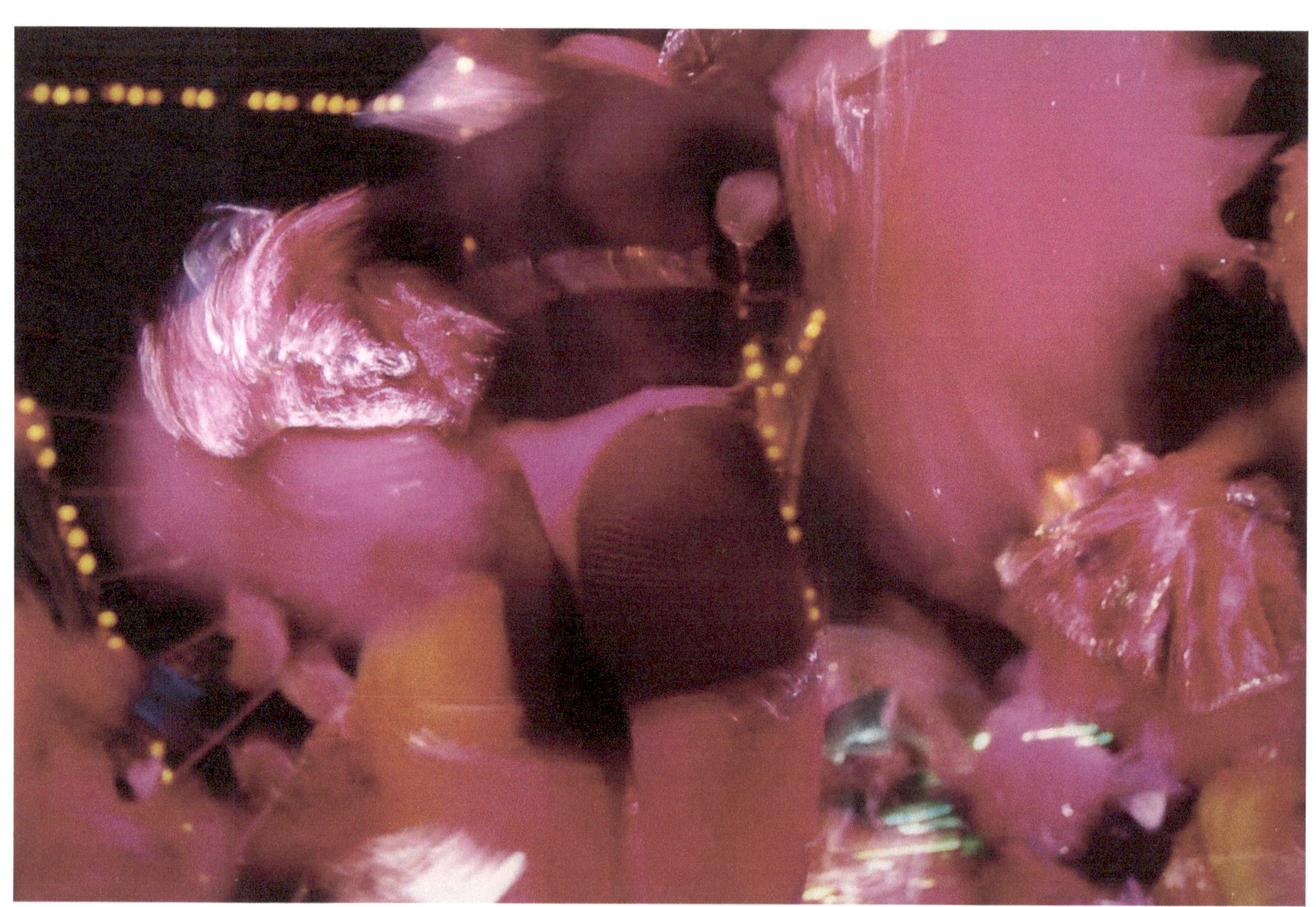

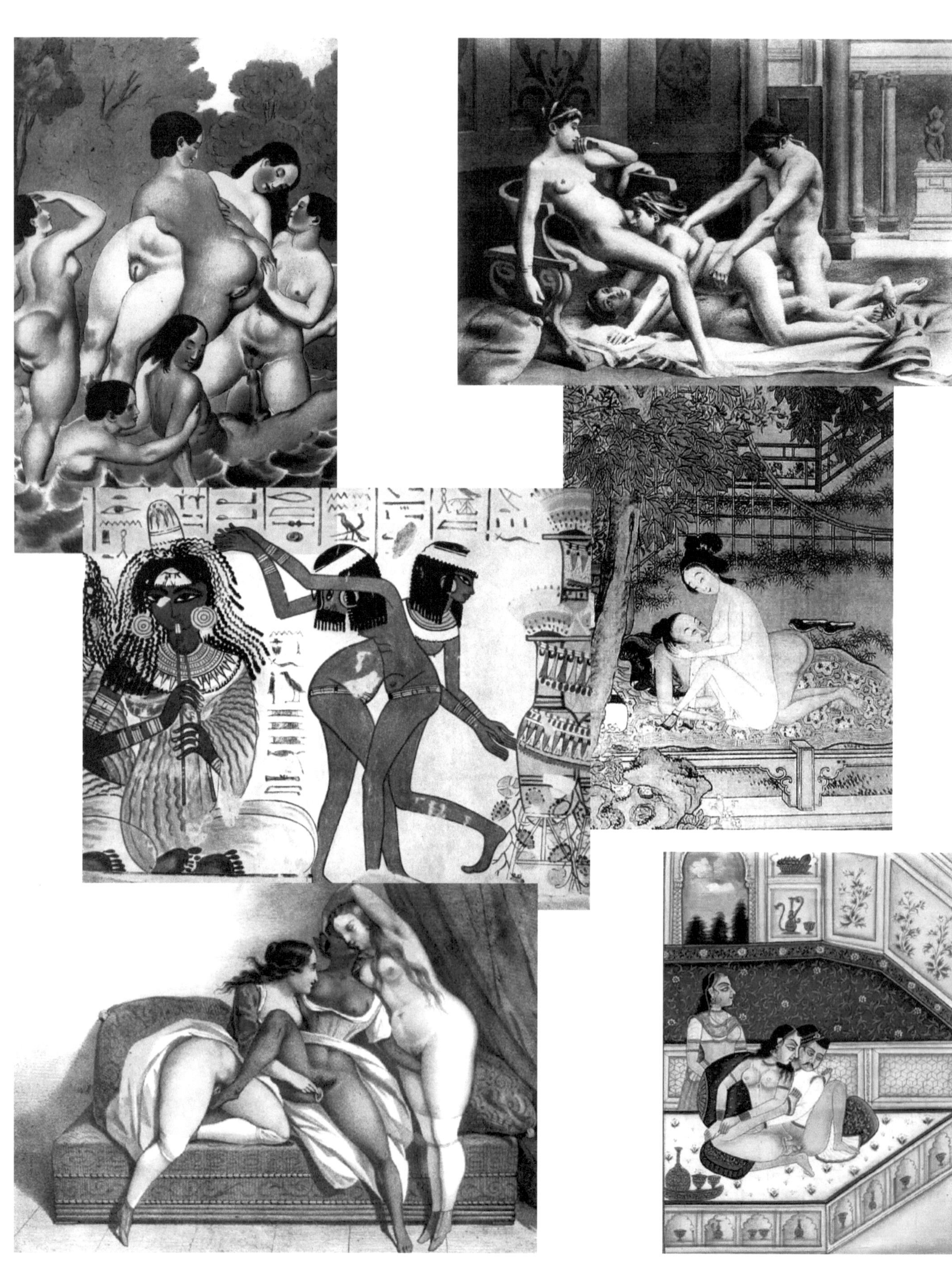

...an affirmation of our birthrights as a people of both, the stars and of the earth, and all the mysterious qualities contained therein... ...orgiastic chaos and creation that will not be contained but can be directed... ...a reminder that the source of creation resides within... ...a celebration of independent, powerful and sensual feminine energy that seeks to create without hurting or controlling anyone... ...a challenge to and a shift in the powers that be... ...the arrival of the seven sisters navigating the divine ships through chaos and creation...

...qualities such as...

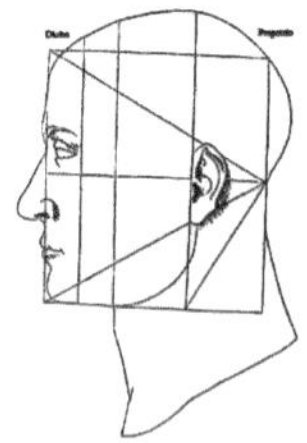

creating all of life's experiences deliberately

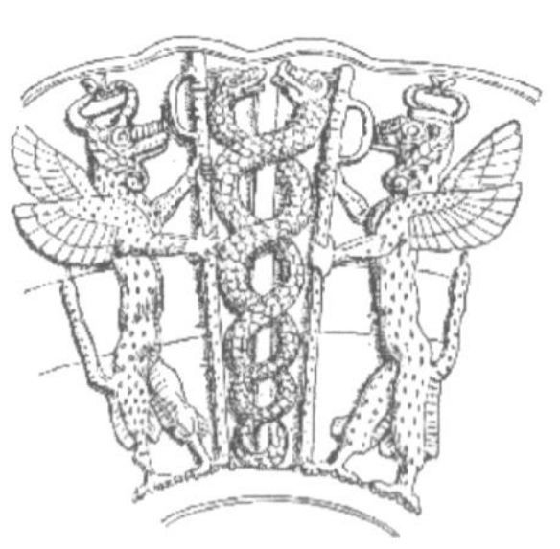

expressing genes according to your will

healing yourself or another instantly or gradually

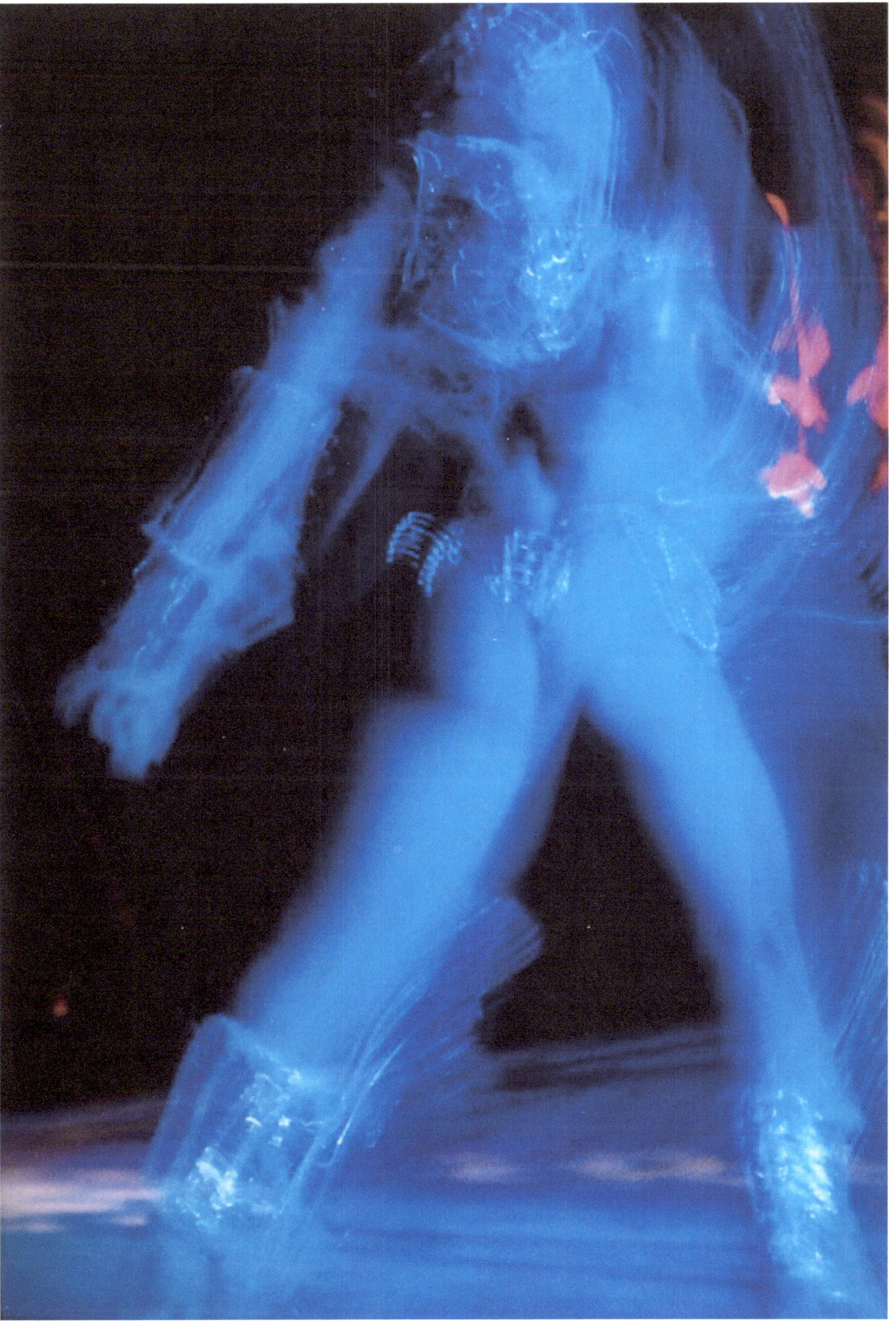

...qualities such as...

feeling one with the heart of all creation

...qualities such as...

Φ   1.61803399

knowing when someone tells the truth

tasting immortality

holding both sides of a paradox until something completely new emerges

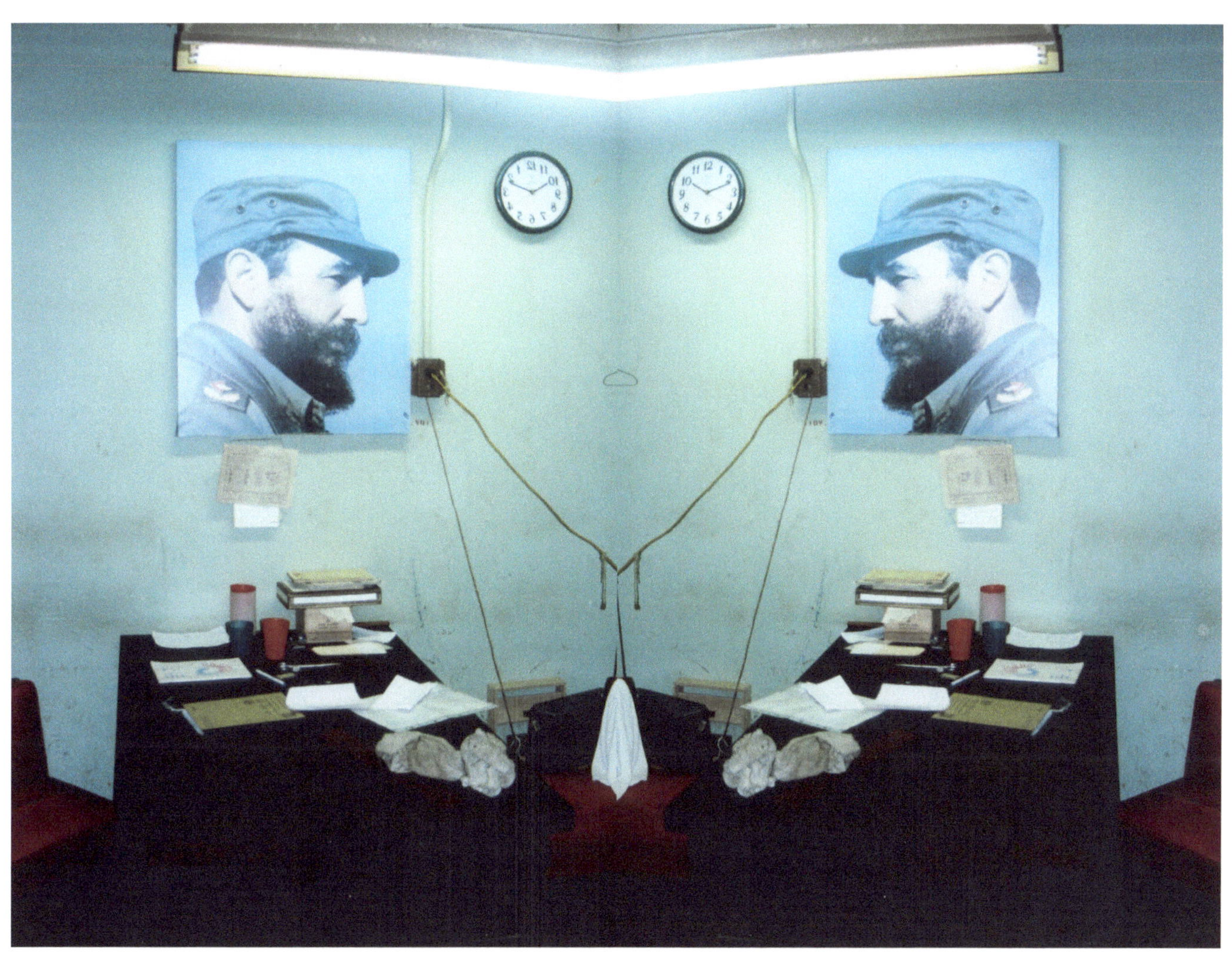

talking with trees

...qualities such as...

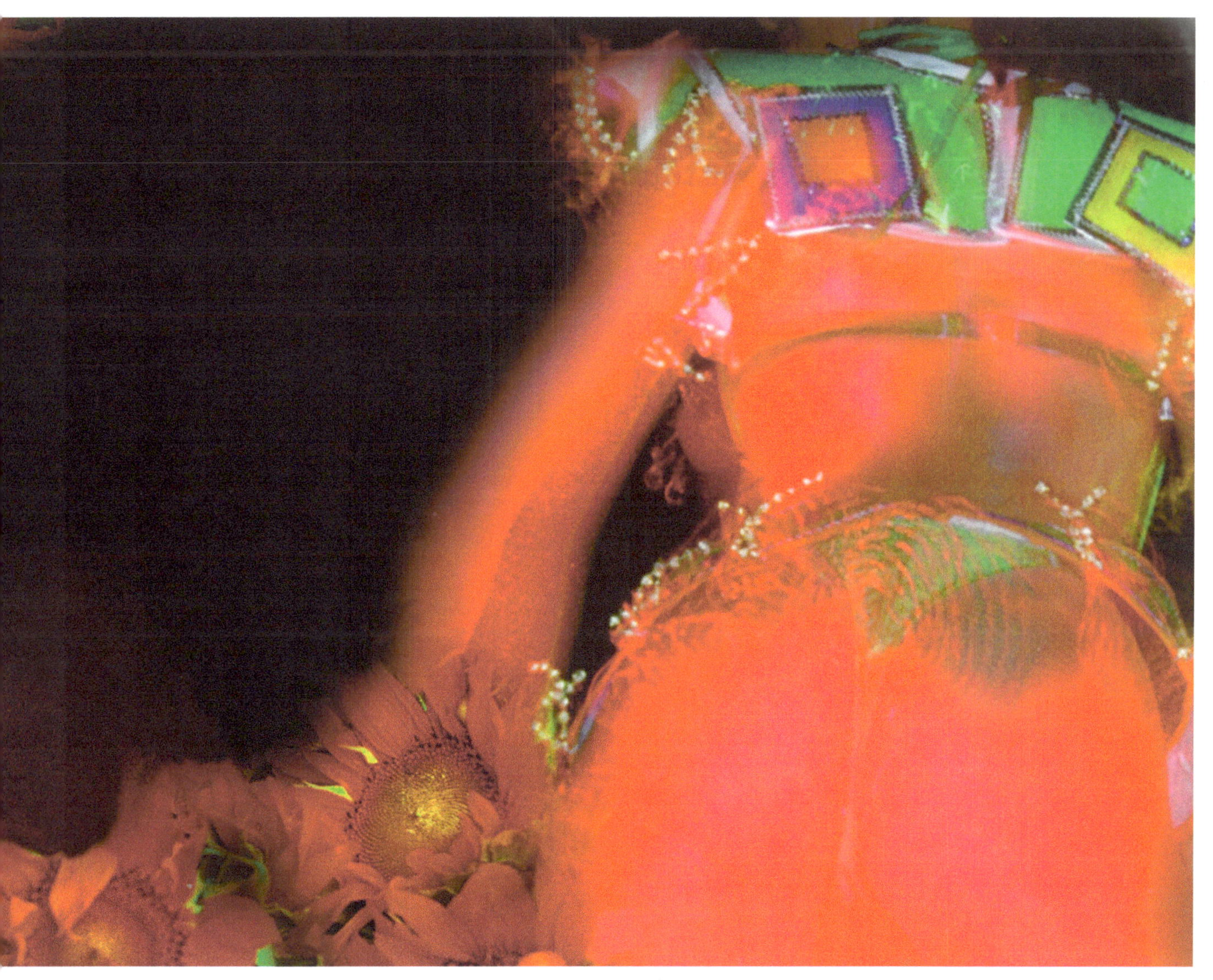

playing in other worlds...

Carnival always has a local flavor and while similar carnival themes can be found in a thousand different festivals around the globe, carnivals, which contain several of the themes discussed in this book are celebrated in specific cities and regions in the countries of:

Antigua (Carnival)
Argentina (Carnaval)
Aruba (Carnival)
Austria (Fastnacht, Fasching, Karneval)
Belgium (Karnaval)
Bolivia (Carnaval)
Brazil (Carnaval)
Colombia (Carnaval)
Croatia (Karneval, Maskare)
Cyprus (Apokrea, Kreatini and Tyrini)
Czech Republic (Masopust)
England-London (Carnival)
Germany (Karneval, Fasching, Fastnacht)
Ecuador (Carnaval)
France (Carnaval)
French Guiana (Carnaval, Touloulous)
Greece (Karnavali)
Honduras (Carnaval)
India (Holi)
Italy (Carnevale)
Japan (Asakusa)
Macedonia (Carnival)
Malta (il-Karnival ta' Malta)
Netherlands (Carnaval, Vastelaovend)
Netherland Antilles (Carnaval)
Nicaragua (Carnaval, Alegria por la vida)
Panama (Los Carnavales, Carnaval)
Peru (Carnaval)
Philippines (Sinulog)
Portugal (Carnaval)
Russia (Maslenitsa)
Slovenia (Kurentovanje)
Spain (Carnaval)
Switzerland (Fastnacht, Karneval)
Trinidad and Tobago (Carnival)
Uruguay (Carnaval)
Venezuela (Carnaval)
United States (Carnival, Mardi Gras, Burning Man, Halloween)

Cuba on Fire

The Film's Narrative (Written in 1999)

Cuba is the largest of the many islands that string like pearls through the warm blue waters of the Caribbean Sea. She has captured the imagination of revolutionaries, Nobel Prize winners, pirates, writers and thousands of friends from all over the world. Ernest Hemingway's, The Old Man and the Sea, was set in Cojimar just outside of Havana. Winston Churchill, Graham Greene and Ava Gardner fell in love with Cuba.

In fact falling in love with Cuba is so common among those who visit the island that it is almost considered epidemic.

The romance with the spirit and soul of Cuba is ageless, and perhaps an ancient

magic is its driving force. It can been seen between the stately Spanish columns, in the quiet courtyards of Old Havana, it can be noticed in the lively streets of Camaguey, and it can be felt on the warm ocean breeze blowing over the Catalan tiled roofs, the Creole patios, and the wrought-iron balconies. This force is in the blood of Cuba, and its pulse can be heard in the many famous rhythms born out of it. It flows throughout the Mambo, the Rumba, and the Chachacha, beckoning the pelvis to gyrate.

But historically nowhere can it be noticed more than at the end of winter, when the sweet pollen of the tropical flowers are carried by the winds of time to announce new life. When a festival as old as spring itself celebrates the reemergence of spring. When it is the time of the Carnival.

Like blood pulsing joyfully through the veins of a dancing heart, a great explosion of sensual colors, rhythms, music and dance flows through the many streets in the city of Santiago de Cuba. Humor, play, music and dance blend with expressions of the spiritual. These images and rhythms of Cuba's passion infiltrate the imagination of anybody living in or visiting the island nation. The ancient traditions are alive and weave themselves into the fabric of life. In the hot and humid air this unique and grand celebration gives form and expression to that force that romances Cuba's spirit and soul.

These striking images from Santiago de Cuba are very similar to those of carnivals from other places in the world and can also be found throughout many recorded histories. They raise some interesting questions about where these traditions originated, and why they draw millions of people to similar festivals all over the world.

As ancient legend has it... "In the beginning, before eternity, before space, before creation itself there was no sun and there was no moon, the earth was without form, and void: and darkness was upon the face of the deep." In the beginning was the great mother, the formless one and her cloak was the sea of darkness and her veil was the night. Omnipotent and able to create all the universe by herself, she preferred

to create together... and so she ripped her cloak and opened her veil and she created god. And together they spoke the words of creation. And the words immediately became our universe and all the many worlds and beings in it."

Chaos is said to be her cloak and it has many names. It is the underworld; it is called a place of death, a place of birth. It is the journey into the unconscious that our conscious mind cannot comprehend.

Her sons and daughters celebrate the death of the old and the birth of the new in the celebration of the crazy and chaotic time of carnival.

The carnevalistas change themselves and enter into this realm of chaos and emerge rejuvenated, healed from the toll of daily rut and routine; they emerge with new understandings, powers, strengths, and realized talents. Carnival is the caterpillar, the cocoon and the butterfly all at once.

Carnival begins by recreating the primordial chaos out of which raw creative energy erupts, and in time change emerges. It begins by holding paradoxes like death and birth equally and at the same time. Yin and Yang, good and evil, harmony and dissonance are woven masterfully into the frenzy, through music and rhythm, by wearing masks, body paint, headdresses, and costumes. In Carnival anyone is free to create the outfit that best fulfills the need of their inspiration. You can be king or queen, you can be death, or a fearful warrior, you can dress or not, and be as sexy as you want to be.

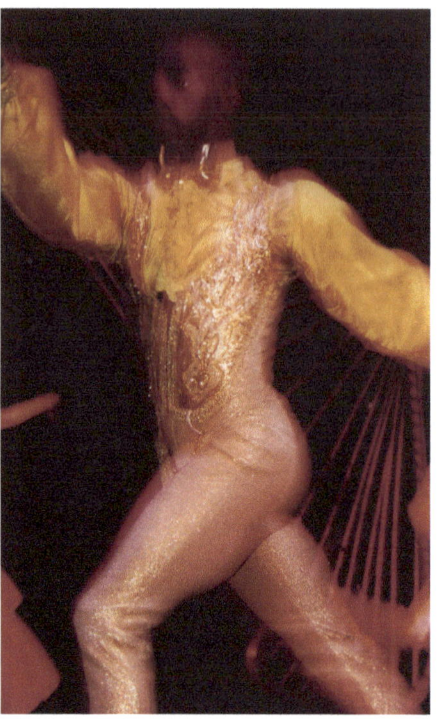

With this freedom, we remember that we all are children of the goddess. We remember the power to create the life we want is within us. We remember to choose our destiny, we make it fun, and we know we are so much more than meets the eye. This we know is at the core of the carnival mythology. Dance and music become a prayer of the divine power streaming forth from all, spilling into the streets, blending with the sweat, the hot, and humid air in this glorious night in Santiago de Cuba.

In the beginning of Christianity, pagan or "heathen" worship coexisted with Christianity for many centuries. Either the Christian churches, unable to convert those "heathens", used a clever tactic of absorbing and integrating many of the pagan rituals, images, myths, symbols and holidays into their view on spirituality, or the "heathens" took part in this process to fool the churches. Afro-Cuban slaves who were forced to abandon their African deities for the sake of worshiping the Christian god used the same tactic to continue their ancient ways. For example, during processions, the altar of sword carrying Santa Barbara was carried through the streets, yet, beneath it was an image of Shango the African lord of thunder and lightning, lord of drumming and dancing, and the epitome of male beauty. With time the two images merged, which are now sacrosanct.

The carnevalistas play, have fun and with great humor shout out: "look at us, look at us, no matter what you believe about how life works, how can it contain all the limitless possibilities?" "I am more than meets the eye, I am something more, look through my funny shape". Sing with us the ancient song, claim oneness with nature, claim the power of creation, we are having fun being magical, we direct the shape of our lives. The death of winter, the birth of spring; it is in us, a transcendence of the self-centered human being into one of spiritual dimension and abilities.

The Greek goddess Semele, while she was pregnant with Dionysus, felt an untamed lust to dance whenever she heard inspired music. So the unborn Dionysus danced safely, deep inside her being. In the transformation of birth, Dionysus thought his mother had died. So he followed her into the underworld to look for her. There he ate the sacred ambrosia, emerged in a boat from the mouth of an enchanted cove facing the deep blue sea.

In ancient Greece hundreds of years before Christ, the ship of Dionysus was pulled on wheels through the streets. It was followed by sensual, untamed processions of music and dance, harmonic and dissonant at the same time. Tonight the archetypal Greek myth of Dionysus transforms into a current Cuban reality. Although carrozas are a newer expression for the carnival in Santiago de Cuba, they are the Dionysian ships of today. They are ships in which, like thousands of years ago, splendid dancers sway their hips to celebrate the feminine source of all life.

The city of Santiago de Cuba has a long carnival tradition that reflects the many different cultural influences present throughout the history of their neighborhoods. European influences are from Portugal, Spain, France and England. There are also Indian influences. As well as Creole, Chinese, and themes of the West Indies, especially Haiti. But here no influence is stronger than that of Africa.

Santeria the Blending of Christianity with the Orishas Yoruba-based traditional African religious worship has blended with that of Christianity, which is now called Santeria. The old African Gods are called Orishas. In Santeria the concept of original sin does not exist. The Orishas have strengths, weaknesses and defined characters. There are unique dynamics between the deities reflecting the relationships among the many different human personalities. Dynamics are played out in intricate dances, rhythms and songs teaching metaphorically their inherent wisdom. The Orishas move on the scent of the night, they are heard in the silence between each cord of the traveling rhythms, they are woven into the fabric of every costume, and they are the salt in every drop of sweat.

The contagious rhythms of the drums thunder through the velvet nights, making it impossible not to be moved by them. The dance of creation, carnival, is under way. Thousands of years ago dancers would pound the earth with rhythmic steps in an attempt to wake up spring and thus part take in the sacred dance in the circles of life. Dancers use their feet to tap, they add another beat to the orchestra, their hands clap as their pelvises rotate to the pulsating music, rhythmically weaving a tapestry of the ancient, merging with the passion of today, as if being irresistibly drawn by invisible strings into a future bright and free.

In Santiago de Cuba, the King and dignified advisors of each cabildo, or neighborhood-based carnival group, guide their neighborhoods beneath their flags to parade their music and dance, new and unique each year, to the drums and high-pitched melody of the Chinese cornet. These cabildos reflect common historical and ethnic experiences and provide a source of belonging and positive pride. These groups have been in the past as powerful as the governments of there times and were not to be underestimated in shaping life on the island. Still today they play an important role in defining values in their neighborhoods. In Santiago de Cuba at the time of slavery, on January the sixth, Three Kings Day, the cabildos elected a king from among themselves and together they went to the governor's palace in a grand procession. The Spanish governors of that time received the king and the cabildos and by doing so reversed the social order.

On the European continent and in times more ancient, the king of Carnival was allowed to rule and everybody had to obey him until, like all savior figures, he must die to be reborn again. When his short reign was over the king was literally killed and his body was used to fertilize the fields to assure healthy

and bountiful crops. As Carnival evolved from those violent times, animals were substituted and at other times the king was destroyed metaphorically, such as by the burning of a straw figure. Ultimately the king was devoured as bread and wine representing his flesh and blood. The carnival kings represent mythologically this drama of death and resurrection. They are winter dancing to a deadly tune with the power of spring.

Ironically, as carnival is about the death of the old and the birth of the new, Santiago de Cuba also celebrates the day Fidel Castro and his followers attempted to storm the Moncada Barracks on March 26, 1953, under the cover of Carnival, hoping that Batista's soldiers would be busy with managing security in the streets. It turned out it wasn't much of a help, for Fidel Castro was arrested, tried, and after some years in prison exiled to Mexico. Nevertheless, it marked the beginning of far-reaching changes for this island nation and is celebrated to this day, especially here in Santiago de Cuba.

And so, no matter where Carnival is celebrated, or what form it takes, it always reminds you that it can be fun to be the author of life. That the dances of life, no matter if harmonious or out of tune, no matter how chaotic or crazy or out of control, can be filled with sensual magic, with substance of soul, and with creative flight of spirit.

Picture index: Credit in order of appearance. Pictures with no credits are by author.

Carnival, night. Santiago de Cuba.

Portrait of Friedrich Nietzsche by Hans Olde ~1899. *First appeared in the German magazine "Pan", no. 4 of the fifth year (1899/1900), ca. page 233;* **Reproduction uploaded to Wikimedia Commons on June 29, 2005 by 20050627.**

Illustration by Gustave Doré of 1861 edition of Dante's Inferno. Original uploaded to Wikimedia Commons was Vae victis on May 19, 2006.

Artists rendering of Sirius A and B. The painting was created for NASA, European Space Agency (ESA) by the Hubble European Space Agency Information Centre. Credit: G. Bacon (STScI)

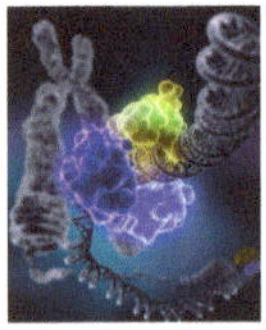

DNA ligase I repairing chromosomal damage. Courtesy of Tom Ellenberger, Washington University School of Medicine in St. Louis. November 21, 2006. National Institute of General Medical Science (NIGMS) United States Federal Government.

John Collier, 'Lilith.' 1892. Original upload to Wikimedia Commons July 2, 2006 courtesy A.I.

Bacchanalia. Auguste Léveque (1864-1921) Originally uploaded to Wikimedia Commons courtesy 'Act' on November 15, 2006.

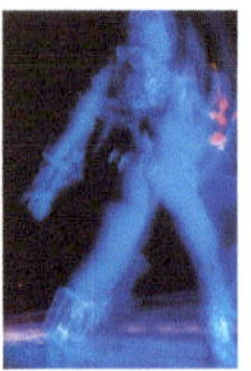

Dancer at the Tropicana Night Club in Havana, Cuba.

Innana, Babylonian Goddess of the Night. Approx. 1792 - 1750 BC. British Museum, London. Uploaded to Wikimedia Commons on January 27, 2007 courtesy Hispalois.

Oil painting entitled Almée by German artist Nathanael Sichel. 1843-1907. Uploaded to Wikimedia Commons May 21, 2005 courtesy Eloquence.

The 'Reception' by English painter John Frederick Lewis. 1805-1875. Uploaded to Wikipedia Commons on March 19, 2008 courtesy Bcrowell.

The meeting of Bacchus and Ariadne. Oil on canvas by Italian Painter Sebastiano Ricci. 1659-1734. Uploaded to Wikimedia Commons on May 21, 2005 courtesy Eloquence.

Upper part of hieroglyphic depiction from the 1st (1876–1899), 2nd (1904–1926) or 3rd (1923–1937) edition of Nordisk familjebok. Wikipedia Commons description: Ett stycke ur Dödsboken, kap 107, Lepsius, 1842. Uploaded January 12, 2007 courtesy Boivie.

Caduceus. Courtesy Rama and Eliot Lash. Wikimedia Commons. March 26, 2006.

Anubis. Courtesy Ningyou. Wikimedia Commons. January 3, 2006

Olmec Head number 6. Museum of anthropology at Xalapa, Vera Cruz, Mexico Uploaded to Wikimedia Commons on 8 August 2006 courtesy Maunus.

Nile Valley. Photo by NASA. Uploaded to Wikimedia Commons on March 26, 2005 courtesy Usuari:Joanjoc

Painting by John Collier entitled *The Land Baby*, 1899. Color altered. Uploaded to Wikimedia Commons on August 21, 2006 courtesy Snotty.

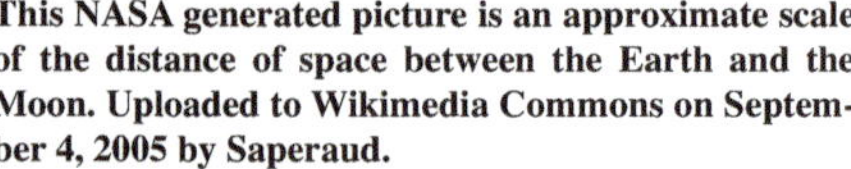

This NASA generated picture is an approximate scale of the distance of space between the Earth and the Moon. Uploaded to Wikimedia Commons on September 4, 2005 by Saperaud.

Radha celebrating Holi, ~1788. (Digitally enhanced version) Kangra, India. Victoria Albert Museum. Author listed as anonymous. Uploaded to Wikimedia Commons June 7, 2008 courtesy Abhishekjoshi.

English Painter John Collier, The Pharaoh's Handmaidens. 1883. Uploaded to Wikimedia Commons August 21, 2006 courtesy Snotty.

Artist: William-Adolphe Bouguereau. Bacchante on a Panther (1855). Uploaded to Wikimedia Commons on February 13, 2005 courtesy Thebrid.

Engraving by French artist Édouard-Henri Avril. (1843-1928) Uploaded to Wikimedia Commons July 22, 2006 courtesy ~Pyb.

This Sun, zodiac, solstices and equinoxes depicting mosaic pavement of a 6th century synagogue at Beit Alpha, Israel was generated by NASA. Uploaded to Wikimedia Commons on March 12, 2006 courtesy Maksim.

Three Generation. Trinidad, Cuba.

One Generation. Santiago de Cuba, Cuba.

Extract from the Cyrus Cylinder giving the genealogy of Cyrus the Great and an account of his capture of Babylon in 539 BC. "Babylonian Life and History", p. 86.1884. By E.A. Wallis Budge. Uploaded to Wikimedia Commons on September 15, 2008 courtesy ChrisO.

Dancer at the Tropicana Night Club in Havana, Cuba.

Dancer at the Tropicana Night Club in Havana, Cuba.

Chars des étudiants au Carnaval de Paris, Mi-Carême1897. Original source reported as Le Petit Journal, supplément illustré, page 109. Uploaded to Wikimedia Commons May 12, 2008 courtesy Basili.

Iron-age rock drawing from Sweden. Uploaded to Wikimedia Commons August 24, 2007 courtesy Fingalo.

German Prince in his carnival float from 1886. Original source from: Friedrich Schütz: Die moderne Mainzer Fastnacht. in: Franz Dumont, Ferdinand Scherf, Friedrich Schütz (Hrsg.): Mainz – Die Geschichte der Stadt. Uploaded to Wikimedia Commons February 3, 2008 courtesy Martin Bahmann.

Joseph Smith Hypocephalus found in the Gurneh area of Thebes, Egypt around the year 1818. Facsimile No. 2 From the Times and Seasons. Uploaded to Wikimedia Commons July 28, 2008 courtesy Magnus Manske.

Postcard of Mardi Gras, New Orleans ca. 1900. Uploaded to Wikimedia Commons January 12, 2008 courtesy Infrogmation.

All images on this page are from the Carnival in Santiago de Cuba.

Dancer at the Santiago Tropicana Night Club in Santiago de Cuba.

Images on both page age from the Carnival in Santiago de Cuba.

Images on both page are from the Carnival in Santiago de Cuba.

Images on both page are from the Carnival in Santiago de Cuba.

Original 1915 caption: "Worship of the Moon God. Cylinder-seal of Khashkhamer, patesi of Ishkun-Sin (in North Babylonia), and vassal of Ur-Engur, king of Ur (c. 2400 BC) (British Museum)." Donald A. Mackenzie, Myths of Babylonia and Assyria (1915), p. 50. Photo: Mansell. Uploaded to Wikimedia Commons on August 23, 2007 courtesy Dbachmann.

Dancer at the Santiago Tropicana Night Club in Santiago de Cuba.

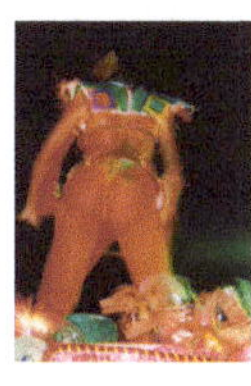

The Pleiades painted by Elihu Vedder in 1885. Uploaded to Wikimedia Commons July 24, 2007 courtesy Pharos.

Float dancers both pages. Carnival in Santiago de Cuba.

Float dancers. Carnival in Santiago de Cuba.

British painter John Collier: Lilith, 1892. Uploaded to Wikimedia Commons October 29, 2007. Courtesy Conscious.

Castillo de los Tres Reyes Magos del Morro; Havana bay, Cuba.

Memeber of Santiago de Cuba cabildo.

Dutch painter Jan van Eyck. "Ghent Altarpiece", detail: Eve. 1432. Uploaded to Wikimedia Commons April 8, 2006 courtesy Piet de Somere

Creation of the Sun and Moon by Michelangelo, face detail of God. 1511. Uploaded to Wikimedia Commons October 30, 2007 courtesy PTaylor

Christopher Columbus and others showing objects to Native American men and women on shore. From the Library of Congress; Lithograph created between 1860 and 1880. Uploaded to Wikimedia Commons May 25, 2005 courtesy ADGE.

Cuban president Fulgencio Batista, 1952 Uploaded to Wikimedia Commons March 9, 2008. Courtesy Zubosud 89.

Fidel Castro addresses delegates of the General Assembly of the United Nations in New York in 1960. Uploaded to Wikimedia Commons February 1, 2007. Courtesy Ejercito Rojo 1967.

Carnival in Santiago de Cuba.

Images on both page ae from the Carnival in Santiago de Cuba.

Asyrien relief. Anzu bird. Uploaded to Wikipedia common April 23, 2009 courtesy DreamGuy.

Portrait entitled 'Dreaming of Flying'.

Santeria initiation; Havana, Cuba.

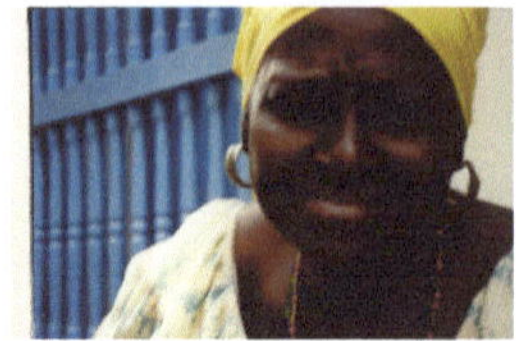

Portrait, Old Havana, Cuba. Courtesy Oreet Rees.

A simple black-and-white version of the Spiral Goddess symbol of modern neo-paganism. Created and uploaded to Wikimedia Commons September 3, 2008. Courtesy AnonMoos.

Dancers at the Tropicana Night Club in Havana, Cuba.

Germanic Goddess Eostre. 1901 by Johannes Gehrts. Published in book *Walhall: Germanische Götter- und Heldensagen* bu the authors Felix Dahn and Therese Dahn. Uploaded to Wikimedia Commons August 27, 2008 courtesy Bloodofox.

Carnivalista from Santiago de Cuba.

Portrait, Grenada, both pages.

Portrait; both pages. Havana Vieja, Cuba.

Portrait, Old Havana, Cuba.

Chromolithograph of a Samoan snake charmer. Printed in the 1880s, the poster gave rise to the common image of Mami Wata, a water goddess of the African diaspora. Uploaded to Wikimedia Commons August 16, 2005 courtesy Amcaja.

Polish painter Pantaleon Szyndler, Eve 1889. Uploaded to Wikimedia Commons September 5, 2006. Courtesy Zana Dark.

Portrait, Santiago de Cuba.

Carnivalista from Santiago de Cuba.

Both pages dancer at the Tropicana Night Club in Havana, Cuba.

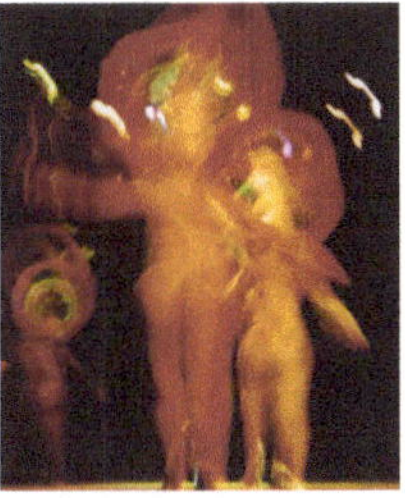

Both pages dancer at the Tropicana Night Club in Havana, Cuba.

Dancer at the Tropicana Night Club in Havana, Cuba.

Franz von Stuck. Wächter dea Paradieses. Uploaded to Wikimedia Commons May 21, 2005. Courtesy Eloquence.

Dancer at the Tropicana Night Club in Havana, Cuba.

Austrian painter Peter Fendi, Scène érotique 1835. Uploaded to Wikimedia Commons October 3, 2005. Courtesy Rama.

Algerian painter Édouard-Henri Avril 1843-1928. Uploaded to Wikimedia Commons July 22, 2006. Courtesy ~Pyb.

Wall painting from a grave in Thebes, Egypt depicting Egyptian dancers and Flutists, with an Egyptian hieroglyphic story. Painter unknown, ca. 1400B.C British Museum. Uploaded to Wikimedia Commons November 18, 2007. Courtesy Jeff Dahl.

Ancient Chinese erotic Painting. Uploaded to Wikimedia Commons January 22, 2009. Courtesy Ewang. chinaontv.

Lesbisches Spiel, anonymous Lithograph ca. 1840. Uploaded to Wikimedia Commons May 10, 2008. Courtesy Mutter Erde.

Kama Sutra Illustration. Author unknown, ca. 1900. Uploaded to Wikimedia Commons November 21 , 2007. Courtesy LostCause1979.

Dancer at the Tropicana Night Club in Havana, Cuba.

Dancer at the Tropicana Night Club in Havana, Cuba.

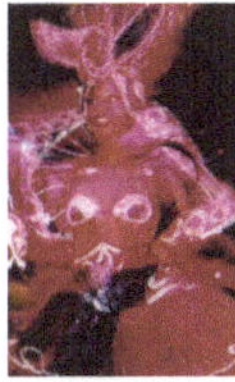

Dancer at the Santiago Tropicana Night Club in Santiago de Cuba.

Both pages dancer at the Tropicana Night Club in Havana, Cuba.

Bacchanalia. Belgian Painter Auguste Léveque (1866-1921). Uploaded to Wikimedia Commons April 10, 2008. Courtesy Magnus Manske.

Dancer at the Tropicana Night Club in Havana, Cuba.

Cupid Disarmed by Antoine Wateau. France 1715. Uploaded to Wikimedia Commons on March 17, 2007 courtesy Bibi Saint-Pol.

Dancer at the Tropicana Night Club in Havana, Cuba.

Innana, Babylonian Goddess of the Night. Approx. 1792 - 1750 BC. British Museum, London. Uploaded to Wikimedia Commons on January 27, 2007 courtesy Hispalois.

Dancer at the Santiago Tropicana Night Club in Santiago de Cuba.

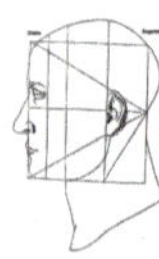

Woodcut from the Divina Proportione, (Golden Ratio) Luca Pacioli 1509, Venice, Italy. Uploaded to Wikimedia Commons on October 4, 2005 courtesy Jossiefresco.

Dancer at the Tropicana Night Club in Havana, Cuba.

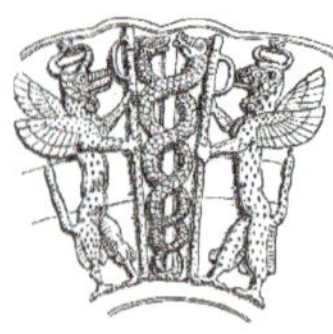

Depiction of the Sumerian serpent god Ningizzida dating from before 2000 BCE. The god itself is the two (copulating) snakes entwined around an axial rod. It is accompanied by two gryphons. Uploaded to Wikimedia Commons January 28, 2007 courtesy Tchoutoye.

Dancer at the Tropicana Night Club in Havana, Cuba.

Caduceus. Courtesy Rama and Eliot Lash. Wikimedia Commons. March 26, 2006.

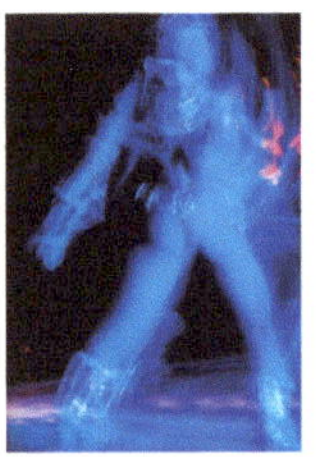

Dancer at the Tropicana Night Club in Havana, Cuba.

Carnivalista from Santiago de Cuba.

The mystical syllable Aum in script. Uploaded to Wikimedia Commons April 5, 2005 courtesy Ranveig

Φ 1 . 6 1 8 0 3 3 9 9

The symbol phi (not pi) represent the golden ratio which is said to be omnipresent in nature and in the heart of all things true and beautiful.

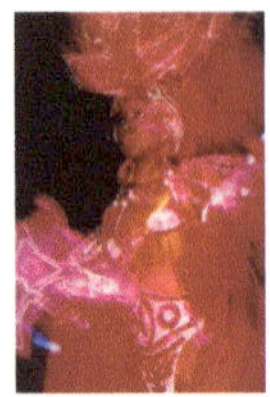

Dancer at the Tropicana Night Club in Havana, Cuba.

Depiction of the Eye of Ra aka 'Eye of Horus.' Authored by ArgentiumOutlaw. Uploaded to Wikimedia Commons December 25, 2006. Courtesy Eleassar.

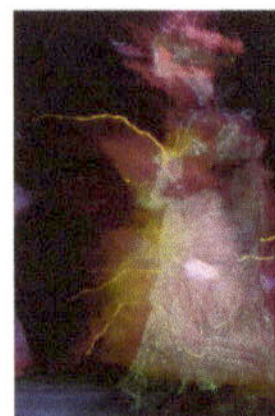

Dancer at the Tropicana Night Club in Havana, Cuba.

Yin-yang symbol or Taijitu created by Kenny Shen. Uploaded to Wikimedia Commons August 23, 2007 courtesy Nyo.

Picture of Fidel Castro on the wall in a Cigar factory Havana vieja, Cuba.

Upper right part of hieroglyphic depiction. Ibid.

Sacred tree left floating while old building is demolished and new is build incorporating three. Havana, Cuba.

Collage of images from the Santiago Tropicana Night Club in Santiago de Cuba.

Pre-revolution classic. Havana, Cuba.

Screenshot of Ava Gardner from the trailer for the film The Killers, 1946. Uploaded to Wikimedia Commons May 24, 2008 courtesy Aylaross.

Fidel Castro addresses delegates of the General Assembly of the United Nations in New York in 1960. Uploaded to Wikimedia Commons February 1, 2007. Courtesy Ejercito Rojo 1967.

Santiago de Cuba.

Image taken by the Hubble telescope and released by European Space Agency and NASA. Uploaded to Wikimedia Commons January 17, 2006 courtesy Ribo.

Image taken from the documentary film 'Cuba on Fire.' Carnevalistas, Santiago de Cuba.

Santeria initiation; Havana, Cuba.

Dancer at the Tropicana Night Club in Havana, Cuba.

Carnival float Santiago d Cuba, Cuba. Image taken from the documentary film 'Cuba on Fire.'

Carnival float Santiago d Cuba, Cuba. Image taken from the documentary film 'Cuba on Fire.'

Image taken from the documentary film 'Cuba on Fire.' Carnevalistas, Santiago de Cuba.

Image taken from the documentary film 'Cuba on Fire.' Carnevalistas, Santiago de Cuba.

Moncada barracks, place of the first battle by Fidel Castro and his revolutionaries, Santiago de Cuba.

Regla harbor, just outside of Havana, Cuba.